LEAP OF FAITH

Frank and Joe pulled themselves onto the hotel roof. "We'd better get out of here before the guys who just crashed into our room figure out where we've gone," Joe told his brother.

Frank pointed toward a door. "That looks like the exit—" Suddenly they heard the sound of footsteps echoing up the stairs, heading for the roof.

"Too late!" Joe cried. "They're already on the way up!"

"Where do we go now?" Frank said. "That's the only way off the roof!"

Joe looked desperately toward the roof of the next building, which looked to be from five to fifteen feet away.

Frank and Joe exchanged glances. Could they make it to the other roof in a single jump? The sound of pounding footsteps from the stairwell told them that they had no choice. Moving as one, the brothers raced toward the edge of the roof—and leapt into space!

Books in THE HARDY BOYS CASEFILES® Series

#1 DEAD ON TARGET
#2 EVIL, INC.
#3 CULT OF CRIME
#4 THE LAZARUS PLOT
#5 EDGE OF DESTRUCTION
#6 THE CROWNING TERROR
#7 DEATHGAME
#8 SEE NO EVIL
#9 THE GENIUS THIEVES
#10 HOSTAGES OF HATE
#11 BROTHER AGAINST BROTHER
#12 PERFECT GETAWAY
#13 THE BORGIA DAGGER
#14 TOO MANY TRAITORS
#15 BLOOD RELATIONS
#16 LINE OF FIRE
#17 THE NUMBER FILE
#18 A KILLING IN THE MARKET
#19 NIGHTMARE IN ANGEL CITY
#20 WITNESS TO MURDER
#21 STREET SPIES
#22 DOUBLE EXPOSURE
#23 DISASTER FOR HIRE
#24 SCENE OF THE CRIME
#25 THE BORDERLINE CASE
#26 TROUBLE IN THE PIPELINE
#27 NOWHERE TO RUN
#28 COUNTDOWN TO TERROR
#29 THICK AS THIEVES
#30 THE DEADLIEST DARE

#31 WITHOUT A TRACE
#32 BLOOD MONEY
#33 COLLISION COURSE
#34 FINAL CUT
#35 THE DEAD SEASON
#36 RUNNING ON EMPTY
#37 DANGER ZONE
#38 DIPLOMATIC DECEIT
#39 FLESH AND BLOOD
#40 FRIGHT WAVE
#41 HIGHWAY ROBBERY
#42 THE LAST LAUGH
#43 STRATEGIC MOVES
#44 CASTLE FEAR
#45 IN SELF-DEFENSE
#46 FOUL PLAY
#47 FLIGHT INTO DANGER
#48 ROCK 'N' REVENGE
#49 DIRTY DEEDS
#50 POWER PLAY
#51 CHOKE HOLD
#52 UNCIVIL WAR
#53 WEB OF HORROR
#54 DEEP TROUBLE
#55 BEYOND THE LAW
#56 HEIGHT OF DANGER
#57 TERROR ON TRACK
#58 SPIKED!
#59 OPEN SEASON
#60 DEADFALL
#61 GRAVE DANGER
#62 FINAL GAMBIT
#63 COLD SWEAT
#64 ENDANGERED SPECIES
#65 NO MERCY

THE **HARDY BOYS** CASEFILES NO. 65

OPERATION PHOENIX NO. 2

NO MERCY

FRANKLIN W. DIXON

AN ARCHWAY PAPERBACK
Published by POCKET BOOKS
New York   London   Toronto   Sydney   Tokyo   Singapore

AN ARCHWAY PAPERBACK *Original*

An Archway Paperback published by
POCKET BOOKS, a division of Simon & Schuster Inc.
1230 Avenue of the Americas, New York, NY 10020

ISBN: 0-671-73101-7

First Archway Paperback printing July 1992

10 9 8 7 6 5 4 3 2 1

Cover art by Brian Kotzky

Printed in the U.S.A.

IL 6+

Chapter

1

"I CAN'T BELIEVE that Dad is dead," said Joe Hardy. His handsome face was set in grim concentration as a salty breeze from the nearby docks ruffled his blond hair. "I thought he could do anything, get out of any situation. And now— now he's gone."

"I know," said his dark-haired brother, Frank, his voice tight and carefully controlled. "I keep hoping I'll wake up and this will all turn out to be some kind of nightmare, only a bad dream. But it hasn't happened."

The two muscular teenagers were standing to one side of the blackened ruins of what had once been Phoenix Enterprises' warehouse in Mombasa, Kenya. Although it had supposedly been a clearinghouse for a legitimate import-export operation, the Hardys had discovered that it was actually a front for the Kenyan arm of a worldwide animal-smuggling operation.

As Joe stared at the ruins he felt only deep bitterness. Twenty-four hours earlier he and his brother watched as their father, private investigator Fenton Hardy, had entered the building as part of their combined investigation of the smuggling operation. There had been an explosion, and then the warehouse had erupted into a flaming inferno. There was no way that Joe or his brother could have saved their father from the flames.

Now, after a sleepless night, Joe and Frank had returned to watch the government authorities comb through the twisted remains of the building in search of survivors. There was no sign of Fenton Hardy, and with each hour it became less likely that he would be found alive.

Finally Joe turned away from the ruins. "It's too late to save Dad's life," he said, "so there's only one thing left to do." He turned to face his brother, his eyes meeting Frank's.

"Right," said Frank, returning his brother's gaze. "We have to find the people who were responsible for Dad's death—and make them pay."

* * *

2

The headquarters of the Mombasa Police Department was only three blocks from the ruins of the warehouse. The Hardys walked the distance quickly, without speaking, and entered the building. Inside, they spoke briefly with the hulking sergeant at the front desk, who directed them down a hallway.

At the end of the hall was an unmarked door with a smoked glass window. Joe knocked twice and waited for a response. A short, middle-aged man with a chestnut complexion and a bald spot on the top of his head opened the door.

"Good to see you boys," said Ranger Pope Rawji, patting Frank on the back. Rawji had been working with the brothers to stop the animal smuggling. "We've been expecting you. The interrogation's already under way, but we're not making a lot of progress. Come on in."

Frank and Joe stepped inside as Ranger Pope eased the door shut behind them. The room was dimly lit and filled with tobacco smoke. In the center of the room was a table. On one side sat a heavyset man wearing a gray business suit and puffing on a large cigarette. Joe recognized him immediately as Rashid bin Said, who until the day before had been manager of the Phoenix warehouse. Joe felt his anger surge at the sight of Said. He worked for the people responsible for killing his father! Opposite Said sat a heavyset, dark-skinned district police official dressed

3

in a crisply starched uniform. He stared at Said through narrowed eyes.

"You realize," the official said to Said, "that even though you refuse to speak, the ranger here and the two young men who just entered the room are working with us. Thanks to them we have sufficient evidence to prove that Phoenix Enterprises has been smuggling exotic animals out of our country in defiance of Kenyan and international law."

Said grinned smugly, waving his cigarette in the air. "So what? The punishment for smuggling animals is no more than a fine and a year in prison, assuming that you can prove these charges. I am not frightened by that. Why should I cooperate with you?"

The police official started to reply, but suddenly Frank Hardy stepped forward. He placed his hands on the table and leaned toward Said. Joe was startled to see the expression on his brother's face. His eyes were entirely lacking in warmth, and his manner was cold and even menacing. When he spoke his voice was harsh. This was unlike the Frank he had known all his life, thought Joe.

"I'll tell you why you should cooperate, Said," Frank said. "Because Phoenix isn't just involved with smuggling. It's involved with murder. The attempted murder of Ranger Rawji here, also that of Oyamo, Keesha, and Dr. Bodine at the Animal Research Compound, and my brother and myself. To say nothing of the actual murder of agent Chris Lincoln from U.S. Customs, who was sent here to investigate your operation, and"—Frank paused for a moment, as though gathering the strength to pronounce the last name—"and Fenton Hardy, my father."

Ranger Rawji stepped to Frank's side. "We also have evidence that Phoenix Enterprises is involved in poaching in the Kenyan bush," he added. "As I'm sure you are aware, Kenyan authorities don't take poaching lightly. My rangers have the right to shoot to kill anyone involved in poaching. No questions asked."

All at once the blood drained from Rashid bin Said's face. He turned to the police official as though expecting him to contradict what Frank and Ranger Rawji had just said. But the official only leaned back in his chair and smiled faintly through tight lips.

"I—I see," Said stammered, the arrogance completely gone from his voice. "I had not realized that things were so serious. Perhaps I can be a little more cooperative."

"That would be good," said the police official. "If you cooperate, perhaps we can see to it that you receive a light sentence. Perhaps, but I make no promises."

"I understand," Said replied. "What is it that you wish to know?"

"One thing," said the official. "Who in Phoenix Enterprises is behind the smuggling and poaching operations?''

Desperation crossed Said's face. ''Please, ask me anything but that! That is the one question I cannot answer!''

''It's the one question you *must* answer, Mr. Said,'' the official said, ''if you wish to save yourself.''

''Why can't you tell us?'' asked Joe. ''Are you afraid that Phoenix will retaliate if you do?''

''No, it is not that,'' responded Said. ''I cannot answer because I do not know. All of my instructions concerning these operations have been by telephone or mail. I have never met or even heard the names of those responsible.''

''You must have some idea where these instructions are sent from,'' the official said.

Said leaned back in his chair and raised his eyes to the ceiling. ''Yes,'' he said. ''I do know where they come from.''

''Where is that?'' asked the official.

''From Stockholm,'' replied Said. ''Stockholm, Sweden.''

''He's telling the truth,'' Frank said. ''Agent Jellicoe said something about going to Stockholm. He mentioned meeting a boss there.''

At the mention of Jellicoe's name, Joe's body tensed. Martin Jellicoe of U.S. Customs had turned out to be secretly working for the poachers, and his betrayal had led to the explosion that had killed the Hardys' father.

Joe leaned close to Frank and whispered in a voice that only his brother could hear. "I guess I know where we'll be going next."

In the hallway outside the interrogation room Frank and Joe paused for a moment with Ranger Rawji as the police led Rashid bin Said to a cell.

"If only I'd been able to decode more of the information in Lincoln's notebook before the police took it away," Frank said bitterly. Frank was talking about Agent Chris Lincoln, who had been killed by Jellicoe and the poachers. Luckily, Frank had found the secret coded notebook that told what Lincoln had learned of the smuggling and poaching.

"There was something in it about 'other merchandise,' and there might have been more information about Stockholm, too."

"Well," said Joe, "there's no telling what other illegal operations Phoenix might be involved with."

"Right," said Frank. "Look at all the weapons and falsified papers they've made available to the operation here in Kenya. Somebody's pumping a lot of money into this smuggling operation, and I have a feeling that the operation doesn't end with animal smuggling."

"That's not for you boys to worry about,"

Ranger Rawji said. "You came here to Kenya to help break up an animal-smuggling ring—and it looks as if you've done what you set out to do. I don't think Phoenix is going to be doing any more smuggling or poaching in this country."

"I hope not," said Joe. "But my brother and I aren't finished. Phoenix may not be smuggling any more animals out of Kenya, but someone in the Phoenix operation was responsible for the death of our father."

"Now it's personal," Frank added.

Ranger Rawji studied the brothers, concerned. He started to reply, but at that moment the door to another interrogation room opened and a pair of police officials stepped out. Joe turned toward the men and immediately recognized the man between them as Martin Jellicoe, in his early forties and of a stocky build.

Jellicoe turned to the Hardys, a smirk on his sunburned face. "Hello, boys. I hope you learned more from our friend Said than these guys did from me. I didn't tell them a thing."

At the sight of Jellicoe's smug expression something snapped inside Joe. He leapt forward to grab Jellicoe by the throat. The customs agent's smirk changed to a look of horror as the younger Hardy pushed him away from the police officials and slammed him against the wall.

"Why, you—" Joe sputtered, his face almost purple with anger. "It's garbage like you, Jellicoe, who killed my father and my girlfriend Iola! I ought to wipe you right off the face of this planet!''

''Hey!'' gasped Jellicoe, making a feeble attempt to push Joe away. ''Get this guy off me! He's gone crazy!''

The two officers with Jellicoe grabbed Joe and pulled him off the terrified customs agent. Ranger Rawji gripped Joe by the arm as the police took the trembling Jellicoe back into custody and led him down the hallway.

''You must remain calm, Joe,'' said Rawji. ''I know how you feel, but there's nothing you can do. The matter is in the hands of the authorities now.''

''Maybe,'' said Joe, not feeling any calmer, ''but there's only so much that the authorities can do.''

A half hour later Rawji dropped the brothers off at a hotel in downtown Mombasa. After they climbed out of the backseat of the ranger's jeep the boys waved goodbye and entered the lobby of the hotel.

After registering, they were led to their room on the third floor by a bellhop. As Frank gave the bellhop a tip, Joe took in their quarters. The room was small, with two beds, a chest of drawers, and a phone.

Joe sat at the end of one of the beds, and Frank took a seat on the other. For a moment they stared at each other in sullen silence. Frank finally spoke. "We can't put it off any longer," he said, his voice heavy.

"I know," said Joe. "We've got to call Mom."

"I'll make the call," Frank offered.

Frank dialed the phone, silently calculating the time difference between Kenya and Bayport. He heard a click on the other end, and the familiar voice of his mother answered, "Hello?"

Fighting to keep his voice from breaking, he explained to his mother as quickly and clearly as possible what had happened. After decades of risking his life in the fight against crime her husband had finally paid the ultimate price—he had died fighting for what he believed in. When Frank finished speaking, there was nothing but silence from the other end of the line. When his mother finally did speak, she sounded calm and self-possessed.

"I'll come to Kenya right away," she said. "I'll take care of all the details when I arrive."

"No, Mom," said Frank. "There's nothing for you to do here. Joe and I are leaving tomorrow."

"You're coming home?" Mrs. Hardy asked.

"No," said Frank. "We have business."

"Let me talk to her," said Joe, motioning for Frank to pass the phone to him. He took the receiver and spoke to his mother in urgent tones. "Mom, Frank and I know what we're doing.

10

Dad left some unfinished business when he died, and we're going to take care of it for him."

"You're all that I have now," said Mrs. Hardy, a distraught note beginning to enter her voice. "I can't let you go running off and risking your lives. After what's happened to your father, I don't think I could take it if something happened to you and Frank."

"We know how to take care of ourselves, Mom," said Joe. "You have to trust us. There are things we need to do."

There was more silence from the other end of the line. Before his mother could reply, Joe said, "We'll talk to you later, Mom. Goodbye." He hung up the phone and returned it to its place on the night table next to the bed.

For a long moment neither brother spoke. Joe raised a questioning eyebrow at Frank.

"You know, big brother," he said, "you did something earlier that surprised me."

"What was that?" Frank asked.

"When I flew off the handle back at the police station and tried to clobber Jellicoe," Joe said, "you didn't try to stop me, as you usually do. You didn't tell me that I had to play by the rules."

"Rules?" said Frank, his eyes taking on an intensity Joe had never seen before, an intensity that sent chills down Joe's spine. "What rules? These guys killed our father. This time there are no rules."

Chapter

2

FRANK HARDY STARED OUT of the airplane window at the city below. Bright redbrick buildings glistened in the sunlight. Between them twisted a series of rivers and canals that meandered right through the middle of the city. To one side Frank could see dark ocean speckled with green islands.

"So that's Stockholm," Joe said, craning his neck to see over Frank's shoulder. "I thought there'd be more—more—"

"Ice and snow?" asked Frank.

"Well, yeah," said Joe. "When you think of Scandinavia, what do you think of? Snow, right?"

"It's summer," Frank pointed out. "Even Sweden thaws in the summer."

"Oh," Joe said dully. "I hadn't thought of that."

Frank was surprised at his brother's refusal to continue their conversation, but he shouldn't have been. Joe was filled with nothing but fury at his father's death. He was unable to concentrate for more than a few minutes at a time.

The airplane bumped once as it contacted the landing strip at Arlanda Airport, then taxied to a halt at the international terminal. Frank and Joe grabbed their duffel bags from the overhead rack. Joe slung a backpack over his shoulder and hurried to the forward exit, Frank just behind him.

The international terminal was clean and old-fashioned, and oddly reassuring. Once inside, a uniformed official directed the brothers toward customs, where a bored-looking official glanced at their passports. His face lit up when he noticed their names.

"Ah, you are the Hardy brothers from America!" he said. "We have been waiting for you!"

Frank's back stiffened. Was there going to be some kind of trouble?

"Don't tell me you've heard of us in Sweden," he said.

"We have been asked to keep an eye out for you," the officer said. "The man over there would like a word with you."

He gestured toward a balding middle-aged

man in a gray suit who was seated in a molded plastic chair, reading a newspaper in English. Overhearing the conversation, the man folded his paper and placed it on the chair next to him. He rose and walked toward the Hardys.

"Hello, Frank, Joe," the man said, holding out his hand for Frank to shake. "I'm agent Jack Fairchild of U.S. Customs. I was told you might be on your way to Stockholm. I understand you helped out with our problem in Kenya.

"I'm sorry about your troubles with Jellicoe," Fairchild continued. "I have to admit that I was shocked." A sad expression crossed his face. "I'm also very sorry about what happened to your father. By the way, why did you take off so suddenly from Kenya? You're not thinking of trying to track down your father's killer, are you?"

Joe gave the customs agent a look of wide-eyed innocence. "No. We just felt we needed a vacation—somewhere far from Kenya."

"And Stockholm is about as far away as we could get," Frank added.

"I'd be insulted if I thought you really expected me to believe that," Fairchild said. "I guess it's your business what you're doing here, but you shouldn't have left Kenya. You're material witnesses in the murder and smuggling case against Phoenix Enterprises. You'd better be back in Kenya in time for the trial."

"The authorities didn't try to stop us when we left," Joe commented.

"The Kenyans think you're American agents," Fairchild told him, "so they treated you with kid gloves. But the American authorities want you back in Kenya as soon as possible. Understand?"

Frank nodded. Although Fairchild probably had the authority to bounce the brothers out of Stockholm, he was relieved that the agent wasn't doing so. Not yet, anyway.

"We understand," Frank said. "We'll be back in Kenya as soon as we're finished with our, uh, vacation here in Stockholm."

"Glad to hear it," Fairchild said, though Frank noticed that the agent raised his eyebrow slightly to indicate that he still wasn't buying the Hardys' story. "Now, can I give you boys a ride somewhere? Stockholm's a big city, and you don't want to get lost."

"Uh, that's okay," Joe said. "We thought we'd just take a cab and do some sightseeing. We don't have any real plans yet."

"Lots of luck," Fairchild said. "In my experience, Swedish cabs are the most expensive in Europe. I hope you brought lots of money."

"We came prepared," Frank said.

The customs agent nodded and started to walk away. "If you need to talk to me," he said, turning back, "you can contact me at the U.S. Embassy. Don't hesitate to call."

"We won't," Frank told him.

"Speaking of money," Joe said after Fairchild left the terminal, "I guess we'd better pick up some local cash."

"Right," Frank agreed. He had noticed a small booth near the walkway to the main terminal. He and Joe pooled their money and handed the large wad to a man behind the counter, who handed them back an even larger wad of Swedish kronor. Frank and Joe split the pile of bills between them.

The international terminal was connected to the main terminal by a long covered walkway. There was a cab stand outside the front door of the main terminal. A smiling taxi driver waved the brothers toward his vehicle. Frank and Joe tossed their backpacks and duffel bags into the backseat, then climbed in after them.

As the cab pulled away from the airport Frank checked over his shoulder and saw a plain black car start after them. He nudged Joe and pointed it out to him.

"You think that's Fairchild?" asked Joe.

"Yeah," Frank said. "He's not going to let us out of his sight for a single minute."

Joe tapped the driver's shoulder. "See that car behind us? Think you can lose him?"

The driver, a baby-faced young Swede, laughed at Joe's request. "You Americans! You watch too many spy movies!"

He stomped on the accelerator, and the brothers were instantly thrown against the backseat of the cab. Frank turned around to watch the black car. It was rapidly falling behind them.

The driver pulled the cab out onto the main highway that ran by the airport, then almost immediately turned onto a small road that led into a thick stand of trees. After driving about a mile down the tree-lined road he made a hairpin turn onto another road that led straight back to the main highway.

As they turned back onto the highway Frank looked around. The black car was nowhere in sight.

"I think you lost him," Frank said. "Good work!"

"No problem," said the driver, winking at Frank in the rearview mirror. The wink, Frank suspected, meant that the driver expected a big tip when they arrived in Stockholm.

It was a long drive into the city. As the brothers discussed what they were going to do Frank pulled a sheet of paper from his shirt pocket. A name and address were printed on it.

"I got this from international directory assistance back in Kenya," he said, handing the sheet to his brother. "Recognize the name?"

"Mike Ryan?" said his brother, reading the name. "It sounds familiar."

"It ought to," Frank said. "He's an old friend of Dad's. A newspaper correspondent for one of the American wire services. I thought I remembered that he was based in Stockholm—and it turned out I was right.''

"Of course!" cried Joe, snapping his fingers. "How could I forget?"

"I figured if anybody could give us help finding our way around Stockholm, Mike Ryan could," Frank said.

As they entered the city, Frank gave Mike Ryan's address to the cabdriver. The driver steered the car through the midday Stockholm traffic. Frank leaned back in his seat and watched the scenery go past. Most of the buildings in downtown Stockholm were imposing red-brick structures that looked as though they must have been built in the middle of the eighteenth century. Every now and then, however, he caught a glimpse of a modern glass-and-steel skyscraper, a sharp reminder that the brothers hadn't taken a sudden trip back through time.

The cab finally pulled up to the curb in front of a long row of apartment buildings. Frank almost gasped when the driver quoted him a fee for the trip from the airport, but he silently handed him a small pile of kronor, which included a generous tip for the driver's help in shaking agent Fairchild's tail.

Mike Ryan's apartment was on the top floor of the middle building in the block. Frank hoped he was at home and buzzed him from the front door. He announced their names through a speaker set into the wall. There was a brief pause, then he heard only a beeping noise, no human voice, as the front door was electronically unlocked. They pushed their way inside and climbed several flights of stairs to Ryan's apartment door.

"Frank and Joe Hardy!" Mike Ryan exclaimed as he opened the door. Mike was a big, good-looking man in his late forties, with reddish brown hair and twinkling blue eyes. "It's been years! Why, I haven't seen you two since you were—what, ten years old? Come on in!"

Ryan waved the brothers inside with his left hand, in which was clasped an unlit pipe. Frank looked around as he stepped through the door. The living room was spacious, with a high ceiling. Books and stacks of old papers were piled about everywhere. Near the windows sat a large wooden desk with a word processor on top. The blinking cursor and glowing green text told Frank that Ryan had been working when they arrived. Frank glanced at the screen long enough to see that Ryan was writing a story about black market arms smuggling.

"What brings the two of you to Stockholm?" Ryan asked as he motioned the boys toward a sofa with thick cushions. "You didn't bring your father with you, did you? What is old Fenton doing these days?"

"That is the reason we're here in Stockholm, Mike," said Frank quietly. He explained briefly what had happened to their father.

Mike Ryan looked as though someone had punched him in the stomach. He staggered backward as though in a daze and sat heavily in a chair. "I can't tell you how sorry I am to hear this," he said in a gravelly voice. "Fenton was one of the finest men I've ever known."

"Thanks, Mike," Joe said. "We hoped maybe you'd be willing to help us catch the people responsible for his death."

A steely look entered Ryan's eyes. "I'll do anything I can," he said. "What do you need done?"

"The organization Dad was investigating in Kenya is called Phoenix Enterprises," Frank explained. "They seem to be based here in Stockholm."

"Yes, I'm familiar with them," Ryan said. "In fact, I just read about the poacher bust in Kenya on the wire service. Of course I had no idea you and your father were involved."

"Yes, we were, and someone in Phoenix is behind Dad's killing."

"We'd like to find out who," Joe added.

Frank and Joe quickly filled Ryan in on the details of their Kenyan adventure. Finally Frank mentioned Chris Lincoln's notebook.

"I managed to decode a few paragraphs of it before the police took it away," Frank said. "Many of the words were scrambled. I remember one word in particular, though. Actually, it was only part of a word. It may have had something to do with Stockholm: *orsenb*. Do you have any idea what it might mean?"

"*Orsenb*," Mike repeated. "No, I don't. But I'll keep it in mind."

"So," said Joe, "do you think you can help us get in touch with some of the European heads of Phoenix Enterprises?"

"I think I can manage that," Mike said. "Just give me a couple of hours to make some phone calls. Do you guys have a place to stay here in town?"

"No," Frank said. "We were hoping you could recommend a hotel."

"Someplace cheap," Joe added. "I think all our money's going into cab fares."

Ryan laughed. "I know just the place. It's in the middle of Stockholm's old town district, Gamla Stan. The area is straight out of the Middle Ages. You'll love it."

"Just as long as our room isn't straight out of the Middle Ages," Frank said.

The newspaperman wrote down the name and address of a hotel on a scrap of paper and handed it to Frank. After promising to get back to them as soon as possible, he led them to the door.

Back on the street Frank waved at a passing cab. As the taxi pulled up to the curb, Frank turned to his brother to motion him inside.

Frank blinked. Something was wrong. In the

middle of Joe's chest was a bright, glowing red dot.

Frank blinked again, and the dot didn't go away. What in the world? He was sure that he'd seen a dot like that somewhere before. In fact—

"Joe!" he screamed. "Look out!"

Suddenly there was the crack of a gun in the distance. Joe lurched forward and fell to the ground—where he lay deathly still!

Chapter

3

FRANK DIVED TO THE GROUND next to the waiting cab. When there was no repetition of the gunfire he crawled up next to his brother.

Joe lay motionless on the sidewalk, his eyes closed. Frank reached out and touched his shoulder.

One of Joe's eyes fluttered open. "Is it safe to get up yet?" he whispered.

"Whew!" gasped Frank. "I thought you'd bought it that time."

"No way," said Joe, "but I think my backpack may be down for the count."

Frank glanced at the green khaki backpack that Joe wore slung over his shoulder. Sure enough, there was a gaping hole in one side of it, revealing one of Joe's old shirts inside.

"Let's get out of here," said Frank. He and his brother leapt to their feet, yanked open the door to the cab, and climbed inside. Frank said something to the driver about his clumsy brother taking a fall, hoping that the driver hadn't connected the sound of the distant gunshot with Joe's behavior. Then he gave him the address of the hotel in Gamla Stan. The driver pulled away from the curb, and Frank and Joe settled back with relief.

"Looks like our visit to Stockholm is starting off with a bang," Joe said.

Fifteen minutes later they arrived in Gamla Stan, which turned out to be a quaint little area of Stockholm situated on a small island in the middle of the city. The island was connected by bridges to the rest of the city, but once on the island Joe really did get the feeling that they had traveled back in time. The streets were so narrow and twisty that only a few were open to cars—the rest were for pedestrians only.

"I'm afraid you must get out here," the driver said in a thick Swedish accent. "I can get no closer to your hotel."

"Okay," Frank said, climbing out of the cab. "We'll walk the rest of the way."

Asking directions, Frank and Joe traveled up a narrow, winding street lined with boutiques and antiques shops and jammed with tourists. The hotel that Mike had told them about was a narrow building between a café and an antique shop. It appeared to be about two hundred years old. Inside, however, Joe was surprised at how clean and spacious it was. Frank checked in at the front desk, passing another wad of kronor to the desk clerk, then he and Joe were taken to a small room on the eighth floor.

Joe looked around at the accommodations. The room was paneled in dark wood, with two brass beds on opposite sides of an old oak table. An ornately carved mirror almost covered one wall of the room.

"Let's take a look at that backpack," Frank suggested, "before your old socks start falling out of it."

Joe stripped off the backpack and dumped it onto one of the beds. The bullet had entered through one side and exited the other. Several items of clothing had been shredded in the process.

"Somebody must have been expecting us here in Stockholm," Joe said. "Somebody besides U.S. Customs, I mean."

"Whoever it is must know what he's doing," Frank said. "That red light on your chest was the beam from a laser scope. Not the kind of thing an ordinary mugger carries around with him."

"But definitely the kind of thing a sophisticated sniper would have," Joe added. "And just maybe that sophisticated sniper works for Phoenix Enterprises.''

''We'll know more when we talk to Mike Ryan again,'' Frank said. ''All we can do now is wait for him to call.''

The Hardys unpacked their belongings and then showered in the small bathroom at the end of the hallway. When they had changed into fresh clothes their phone rang.

''Mike,'' Frank said after he had answered the phone.

''I have some good news for you guys,'' Mike told him. ''I managed to get you and your brother invitations to a lawn party tonight at the home of one of Phoenix's owners, Eleonora Grunewald. She's a rich society lady. I wrote a story about her a couple of years back, and she liked it, though I don't know why. Now I get invited to all her parties. This time I asked if I could bring along a couple of guests.''

''Thanks, Mike,'' Frank said. ''So how do we get there?''

''I'll pick you up at six at the end of your street,'' Mike told him. ''By the way, this is a black tie affair, so you have to rent tuxes. There's a shop two doors down from your hotel where they'll set you up with some fancy duds but won't charge you an arm and a leg.''

Taking Mike's advice, the Hardys visited the small shop that Mike had told them about and rented a pair of tuxedos. At six sharp Joe and

Frank were standing at the curb in freshly pressed evening clothes. Joe stared down at his own clothing in amazement.

"I can't believe I'm wearing this outfit," he told his brother. "Back in Bayport, getting ready for a party means putting on jeans and a T-shirt."

"Yeah," Frank said, "but back in Bayport we don't usually go to parties thrown by millionaire society hostesses."

Mike Ryan pulled up minutes later in a small red car, and the Hardys climbed in. He headed north, crossing a bridge that separated Gamla Stan from the other fourteen islands that made up Stockholm and kept driving toward the edge of town.

"Eleonora Grunewald lives in Sigtuna, which is the oldest city in Sweden," Mike explained. "If you think Gamla Stan is quaint, wait till you see this place. Some of the buildings in Sigtuna go back to the eleventh century."

"This whole country's starting to seem like a museum," Joe said.

"It's not quite that bad," Mike Ryan said, laughing, "but there is a lot of history. Keep your eye out for some of the old abbeys and monasteries in Sigtuna. They can be quite spectacular. Back in the old days people competed to see who could build the biggest church. Some of these places are huge."

The ride to Sigtuna took about half an hour.

Eleonora Grunewald's mansion was located on top of an isolated hill, surrounded by extensive gardens and a large wooded area. As Mike and the Hardys approached the front gate, however, they were greeted by an unexpected sight: Approximately two dozen demonstrators were standing in the middle of the road holding picket signs reading: PHOENIX CRUEL TO ANIMALS and PHOENIX RISES FROM THE ASHES OF INNOCENT CREATURES. Mike flashed his invitation to a guard, who cleared a path through the demonstrators and allowed the car to pass through the gates. Several of the demonstrators hooted loudly at Mike and the Hardys as their car passed them.

"Animal rights activists," explained Mike. "They're pretty angry about that poaching affair in Kenya and Phoenix's alleged role in the illegal importation of animals."

"I don't blame them," Frank said. "If we weren't here to meet the bigwigs at Phoenix, I'd get out and join them."

Mike drove to the top of the hill and parked in an area already half filled with cars. The group climbed out of the car into the almost daylight-bright Scandinavian summer evening. It would stay light most of the night. A tall, elegantly dressed woman talking with a group at the top of the hill noticed Mike and the Hardys approaching.

"Mike!" she cried with delight, leaving her

friends and walking toward the newcomers. "It's good to see you!"

"Good to see you, too, Eleonora," Mike said as she kissed him on the cheek. "I've got some friends I want you to meet. They're the sons of one of my oldest pals."

Frank studied Eleonora Grunewald carefully. She was an attractive but sharp-featured woman who appeared to be in her midforties, with blond hair swept into a towering crown atop her head. Diamond jewelry glittered at her throat, on her fingers, and around one wrist.

"I'm glad to meet you, Ms. Grunewald," Frank said, taking her hand briefly in his.

"Please, call me Eleonora," she said with a smile. "Any friend of Mike's is certainly a friend of mine. I must introduce you and your brother to Ilsa Marie Khoo. I'm sure you'll get along famously."

Frank and his brother were dubious as Eleonora led them and Mike toward a small party of people standing off to one side near the parking lot. All doubts vanished, however, when Eleonora called a young woman to her side and introduced Joe and Frank to Ilsa Khoo.

Joe stared openly at Ilsa, astonished. She was the most beautiful person he had ever seen! Ilsa Marie Khoo was in her late teens, with the high cheekbones of a fashion model. Long, straight black hair framed her jade green, almond-shaped eyes and clear olive skin. She was tall with the athletic body of a Nordic skier. She smiled at Frank when they were introduced but gave a bigger smile to Joe.

Joe smiled back, unable to take his eyes off her.

Uh-oh, thought Frank. My brother has charmed yet another helpless young woman.

Then he noticed the dazed look on Joe's face as he took Ilsa's hand. Maybe, Frank thought, I've got this one backward. Maybe Joe's the helpless one here!

"I'm very glad to meet both of you," Ilsa said in a soft, cultured Swedish accent. "Will you be staying in Stockholm long?"

"Huh?" said Joe. "Oh, we'll be here for a while, I guess. We're not sure yet."

"We just thought we'd stay for a few days and get to know the city," Frank said.

"That's wonderful," Ilsa said. "Then you must let me show you around."

"Perhaps you should introduce me to your friends, Ilsa," said a voice from behind the Hardys.

Frank turned to see a short, muscular man of about fifty standing between him and Joe. His graying hair was cropped short in a military cut above an intense pair of eyes that were strikingly like Ilsa's.

"This is my father," Ilsa said. "Jumsai Lee Khoo. Father, these are the Hardy brothers— Frank and Joe."

Khoo stared intently at the Hardys, as though sizing them up as potential companions for his daughter.

"I'm glad to meet you, Mr. Khoo," Joe said. "Your daughter was just offering to show us around Stockholm."

"Then you must come to visit the Phoenix warehouse while you're seeing the sights," Khoo said. "I'm sure that Ilsa would be happy to give you a tour."

Khoo has something to do with Phoenix? Frank thought. He immediately wanted to know more, so he began to talk with Ilsa's father. He was delighted to learn that Khoo was one of the owners of Phoenix Enterprises. He had been born in Thailand, where he had founded a small import-export firm. But two decades earlier he had moved his firm to Sweden and married a Swedish woman named Ula.

"Ilsa is our only child," Khoo told Frank. "I'm immensely proud of her. She's grown into a lovely and intelligent young woman."

While Frank talked with Khoo he noticed that his brother was deep in conversation with Ilsa.

Frank found himself becoming angry at Joe. Only a few days before their father had been killed. Now Joe was already back to his flirtatious ways!

"I'm afraid there is other business I need to attend to here," Khoo said, perhaps noticing

Frank's momentary distraction. "I hope to see you again tomorrow."

"I hope so, too," Frank told him as Khoo walked off into the crowd.

At that moment Mike Ryan reappeared with a young Swedish man in tow. "I'd like to introduce you to Rutger Linska," he told Frank. "Rutger's an electronics expert and the owner of Diamond Systems. I thought you two might like to get to know each other."

Linska was a small, slender man with the pale complexion and awkward manner of someone who spent most of his time working indoors at a computer keyboard. As Frank introduced himself, Linska's head bobbed up and down nervously and his large eyes blinked rapidly. He stuttered nervously when he spoke.

"I-I'm glad to meet you, Frank," he said. "Mike tells me that you—you might be interested in the work that I do."

"Um, exactly what kind of work is that?" Frank asked.

"I'm—I'm in electronics research and development," Linska said nervously. "I develop aerial guidance systems for jets and missiles."

"Really?" Frank said, wondering if this was why Mike had introduced him to this awkward young man. He had told Mike about Joe's near miss with the laser gun earlier.

"Well, I guess Mike was right," Frank said. "That does sound fascinating."

32

Linska relaxed some when Frank showed interest in his work. "Yes, it is," he replied. "I'm particularly interested in the use of artificial intelligence in guidance systems."

Frank remembered reading something about this topic in a science magazine a few months earlier. "I've heard about that," he told Linska. "The missile has a computerized 'brain' that holds a map of the terrain in its memory. It compares this map with its actual surroundings so that it doesn't get lost."

Linska seemed impressed that Frank actually knew something about the topic. "Why, yes! That's exactly the sort of work I'm involved in! We really must talk about this at greater length," Linska said. "Perhaps you and your brother can visit my laboratory."

"We'd like that," Frank said.

Linska handed Frank a card. "Here's my address. Stop by before you leave Stockholm."

Frank thanked Linska for the card and promised him that he would visit his laboratory. He interrupted Joe to tell him that he was going to wander around and check out the rest of the party.

Frank scanned the grounds. There were several clusters of people on the lawn engaged in animated conversation. A uniformed waiter was strolling around with a tray full of drinks. Frank took a glass of soda from the tray and continued to wander, moving from one conversational group to another, trying to overhear as much as possible.

He didn't hear much. Most of the conversations were in Swedish. What little was in English had nothing to do with Phoenix Enterprises and revolved around the weather, politics, and sports.

At one end of the lawn was the entrance to some kind of garden, bordered by thick shrubs too high to see over. Standing next to the entrance was a wiry man in an ill-fitting tuxedo. He was about thirty, with a dark complexion and piercing black eyes.

"Excuse me," he said as Frank started past him. He spoke in English with a slight Middle Eastern accent. Frank didn't consider it odd that he addressed him in English, since so many people spoke flawless English in Sweden. "I wonder if you could give me a hand. My companion wandered into this hedge maze and seems to have gotten lost. I just got a phone call that we're needed back in Stockholm. I was wondering if you could help me find her."

"Well, sure," Frank said. It was an odd request, but it made a certain sense. Two people could probably locate a missing person in a maze faster than one, assuming that neither of them got lost.

"Did you see which way she went when she entered the maze?" Frank asked. "Maybe you should go that way, and I'll go the other."

"Good idea," the man said, pointing through the maze entrance toward the left passage. "I'll go to the left. Just look for a red-haired woman in a blue dress."

Before Frank had gone more than a few feet he realized that the man who had entered the maze with him was now directly behind him.

Frank started to turn to ask him why he wasn't going to the left when suddenly something was slipped around his neck. Frank tried to pull away but was yanked back.

A piece of piano wire was gripped in the man's hands, and he was tightening it around Frank's neck.

The man, Frank realized, was trying to strangle him to death!

Chapter

4

THE MAN JERKED the garrotte even more firmly around Frank's throat. Frank struggled to get his fingers under it, but the wire was already cutting deeply into his flesh. The man continued to twist it.

Frank had only seconds to get rid of his attacker before he lapsed into unconsciousness! He kicked backward with all his strength, but the man easily evaded the blow and squeezed the garrotte still tighter.

From the other side of the hedge maze Frank could hear the voices of other party goers. But when he tried to cry out, no sound escaped from his throat.

Desperate, Frank twisted his entire body

around to face his attacker in a single sharp movement. The move caught his attacker off guard, and he stumbled for a second, loosening his grip on the wire.

That was all the opening Frank needed. He brought up his left knee and caught the strangler in the stomach. With a sharp exclamation of pain his attacker staggered backward and dropped the garrotte. Frank fell to his knees, still weak from the attack. As he did so the black-eyed stranger pulled a gun from inside his dinner jacket.

"I should have used this in the first place," he announced.

With a sudden burst of strength Frank sprang from his crouched position and drove the top of his head directly into the man's stomach before he could fire a shot. The gun popped out of the man's hands and flipped into one of the thick hedges.

Frank staggered backward, his head throbbing from the impact. He looked up in time to see his attacker start to run for the entrance. Frank shook his head to clear it, then ran in pursuit.

As Frank exited the hedge maze he saw the man dashing across the lawn between knots of party goers.

"Stop that man!" gasped Frank, the words coming out of his throat in a hoarse croak. "He tried to kill me!"

It was too late. The man had already reached the parking lot and was in a large black car.

The engine roared to life, and the car lurched forward—straight onto the lawn!

Frank assumed that the would-be assassin was steering onto the grass to avoid the parked cars in the lot, but his path across the lawn was taking him straight toward the closest gathering of party goers, which included Joe, Ilsa, Mike Ryan, and Rutger Linska. In fact, Frank realized, the car was aimed straight at Rutger Linska!

The Swedish engineer stared at the oncoming car, horrified and apparently frozen in fear. Frank dived straight at Linska, knocking him away as the black car sped over the spot where the engineer had been standing a split second before. Making a wild fishtail turn, the car spun around and headed back toward the road that led to the main gate, tearing up chunks of grass from the lush green lawn. By the time Frank had regained his footing his attacker was already halfway down the hill.

"What was that all about?" cried Joe, rushing to his brother's side. Frank helped Linska, his eyes still wide with shock, back to his feet.

"The guy in that car just tried to strangle me," Frank said.

"Wh-what?" stuttered Linska. "He tried to kill you, too? That's terrible! Why would somebody try to do that?"

"I don't know," Frank said. "I never got a chance to ask him."

Eleonora Grunewald came rushing down the hill from the house with a beefy security guard at her side. "I'm so very, very sorry," she said, sounding genuinely apologetic. "That should never have been allowed to happen."

The security guard briefly questioned Frank in English about the attack and asked if he wanted the police called in. Frank shook his head.

"No, that's okay," Frank told him. "I don't think we need the police. That guy's not coming back."

"It was probably one of those animal-rights protesters," the guard said. "There's no telling what those people will do."

Eleonora Grunewald's eyes flared angrily. "I want you to get rid of those animal-rights people immediately!" she told the guard. "How dare they disrupt my party in this manner? Imagine, one of my guests being attacked in the privacy of my garden!"

"It wasn't that bad," said Frank, purposely downplaying the incident. "He was probably just in a bad mood. Maybe it was something I said."

"Nonetheless," Eleonora said, "I just can't apologize enough. If there's anything I can do to make this up to you, just let me know."

"That's okay, Ms. Grunewald," Frank said. "It wasn't your fault."

"Well, please try to enjoy the rest of the party," Eleonora said.

With that she turned and rejoined the rest of her guests. Rutger Linska wandered off seconds later.

Joe and Ilsa were standing a few feet from Frank. As soon as the others were gone Joe turned to his brother and spoke in a low voice so Ilsa could not hear. "Do you really think it was an animal-rights activist?" Joe asked.

"No way," Frank said. "How many animal rights activists are trained in assassination techniques?"

Joe whistled. "This guy really meant business, huh?"

"Yeah," Frank said. "First he tried to strangle me with a garrotte, then he tried to shoot me with a gun." Frank paused. "Which reminds me, I'd better go see what became of that gun."

"Need help?" Joe asked.

"No," Frank said. "You spend a little more time with your new friend." He nodded toward Ilsa. "I don't think anybody else is going to dare attack us before the party's over."

Frank walked back to the maze as Joe resumed his conversation with Ilsa. As he entered the maze, he glanced around to see if anyone else was inside. He saw no one.

Now, what happened to that gun? Frank wondered. He remembered catching a glimpse of it flying out of the assassin's hands, toward the hedges.

He returned to the spot where their scuffle had

taken place and groped around inside the hedge there. His fingers touched cold metal. He grasped the object and pulled it out. The gun!

Frank made sure that the safety was on and shoved the gun into his pocket. He wasn't sure what he was going to do with it, but he knew that he couldn't leave it. It might also provide a valuable clue to the identity of his assailant.

He headed back to the exit but paused when he heard voices on the other side of the hedge. Two people were standing right outside the entrance having a whispered conversation in English, obviously not wishing to be overheard by just anyone passing by. Something in the tone of their voices caused Frank to stop to listen. After a few seconds he realized that he was overhearing a conversation between Rutger Linska, the Swedish engineer, and Eleonora Grunewald.

"Don't worry," Grunewald said. "The shipment will go through. My people will see to that."

"H-how can you be so sure?" Linska replied, sounding unconvinced.

"I'm always sure," Grunewald told him. "You know that."

"Yes," Linska said, "but you've been out of the country. You've been out of touch with things here in Stockholm.

"Remember," he added, "it was only yesterday that you got back from Mombasa!"

Chapter

5

ELEONORA GRUNEWALD had just returned from
Mombasa? Frank's pulse raced. If she had been
in Mombasa at the time of their father's death,
then she could be one of the people responsible!
At the very least she might know something
about what had happened to Fenton Hardy.

Grunewald and Linska began walking away
from the hedge, and their whispers soon became
inaudible.

After a few moments Frank poked his head
out of the entrance, making sure that the coast
was clear. Grunewald and Linska were nowhere
in sight, so Frank headed quickly back to his
brother and Ilsa.

"Hey, Frank!" Joe said. "Ilsa wants us to

meet her tomorrow morning. She's going to give us that free tour of Stockholm."

"Great," Frank said, grabbing his brother by the arm. "Er, Ilsa, do you mind if I talk to Joe alone for a moment?"

"Certainly not," she replied. "I'm afraid I've been monopolizing Joe all evening. Besides, I'll be seeing you both tomorrow."

"I don't mind, Ilsa," Joe said. "You can monopolize me all you want."

"Later," Frank said, tugging his brother toward a nearby stand of trees. "We've got to talk."

When they reached the trees, Joe looked at his brother with concern. "Okay, so what's up? Did somebody else try to kill you?"

"Not yet," Frank said, "but I just learned something interesting." He told Joe about the conversation he had overheard between Rutger Linska and Eleonora Grunewald.

"Wow!" Joe said. "Eleonora Grunewald sure doesn't look like the type of person who would be behind the Mombasa operation."

"No," Frank agreed. "But looks can be deceiving. Don't forget, she's one of the owners of Phoenix."

"So what do we do now?" Joe asked.

"I think we should check out Grunewald's mansion," Frank said. "Maybe we can find some sort of evidence there that will tie her in to Dad's death."

43

"You mean break into her house?" Joe asked in astonishment. "Don't you think that's a little risky? I mean, the place is crawling with security guards. They'd be all over us in a minute."

Frank stared at his brother. "I can't believe what I'm hearing, Joe. Usually you're the one who wants to jump into action, and I'm the one who's trying to stop you. Well, now I'm not trying to stop you. So what's holding you back? Or are you so infatuated with Ilsa Khoo that you don't care about finding out what happened to Dad?"

Frank regretted the words the moment he said them, but he was too filled with anger to take them back. His brother's mouth dropped silently open for a moment.

"You've got a lot of nerve saying that!" Joe snapped. "How I feel about Ilsa is my own business! You know I care every bit as much as you do about finding Dad's killers!"

Frank sighed. "I'm sorry. I shouldn't have said that. We're both pretty upset right now. Maybe breaking into the mansion is the wrong thing to do. But I do plan to keep my eyes on Eleonora Grunewald."

At that moment Mike Ryan appeared from the direction of the mansion. "Hi, guys," he said. "I'm afraid the party's over. Eleonora has decided to call it a night. I guess the excitement over that guy who attacked Frank was a little too much for her."

Frank gave Joe a sidelong glance and whispered, "Maybe she was just disappointed that the guy didn't succeed."

Mike led them back to his car. Ten minutes later they were on the highway heading back to Stockholm.

"So," Joe asked Mike, "did you learn anything interesting about Phoenix while you were at the party?"

"As a matter of fact," Mike said, "I did. The latest rumor is that Ms. Grunewald is having money problems. It seems she made some bad investments and is now having what is called a cash-flow crisis."

"You mean she's broke?" Frank asked.

"Not far from it," Ryan said. "It's impossible to tell how bad her financial situation really is. I mean, I couldn't go right up to her and ask. I wouldn't get invited to any more parties."

"Maybe she's trying to make up for the money she lost by getting involved with animal smuggling in Kenya," Joe said.

"Yeah," Frank said. "I don't trust this Grunewald woman. I think we should find out a little more about her."

"And maybe we should learn a little more about those animal-rights activists, too," suggested Joe. "I know it doesn't seem very likely that they were responsible for that guy who attacked you at the party, but it wouldn't hurt to investigate a little further."

45

"True, and while we're at it," Frank said, "we might as well investigate Rutger Linska, too."

Frank stuck a hand into one of his jacket pockets and was startled when it touched the metal of the gun. Better not mention the gun to Mike, he thought. Then suddenly he remembered the story he had seen on Ryan's word processor that afternoon.

"What do you know about arms smuggling?" Frank asked Mike. "I noticed that you were writing something about it back at your apartment."

"Kinda nosy, aren't you?" Mike said with a smile. "Yeah, I'm doing a little investigative journalism for the wire service. I'm hoping to put together a five-part series on black market arms dealing. There's an unusually large supply of weapons on the street right now, and nobody knows why. And there are rumors flying that a big underground arms sale is about to go down, maybe somewhere in Stockholm."

"Interesting," Joe said.

Ryan dropped the boys off near their hotel and as Frank and Joe headed back to their room, Joe reminded his brother that they had to get an early start the next day.

"Ilsa expects us to meet her at nine o'clock sharp," Joe said.

"Right," Frank said. "I assume you're planning to pump her for information about Phoenix

46

and its involvement in smuggling operations, right?"

Joe looked hurt. "Well, of course. What else do you think I'm meeting her for?"

"I don't know," Frank said, a sly smile on his face. "But I got the impression that maybe you want to see her because you like her."

"We've got a job to do," Joe said, a defensive tone in his voice. "I figure I can learn a lot from Ilsa, that's all. That's why I was talking with her so much at the party."

"Of course," Frank said with a laugh. "That's what I figured!"

The next morning the Hardys stepped off the bus at a small dock north of Gamla Stan, on the southern edge of the largest of the islands Stockholm was built on, Norrmalm. Ilsa had promised to meet them there.

Joe felt a rush as he saw her step out of a small red sports car and walk toward them dressed in a pair of white nautical-looking shorts and a white shirt. Her hair was swept back into a low ponytail, and a large pair of sunglasses was pushed up on top of her head. Her eyes lit up at the sight of Joe.

"Joe!" she said. "Frank! It's good to see you! I've been looking forward to showing you around the town."

"We've been looking forward to it, too," Joe said. "Haven't we, Frank?"

47

"Oh, right," Frank said. "And I'd like to check out the offices of Phoenix Enterprises, too."

"The warehouse isn't far from here," Ilsa said. "I asked you to meet me here by the docks so I could point out some of the sights to you. You do want to look around, don't you?"

"Point away," Joe told her.

"That's the river Riddarfjärden," she said, indicating the water that flowed past the docks. "It flows right through the middle of Stockholm."

"I hope nobody expects us to pronounce that name!" Joe said with a laugh.

"There sure are a lot of rivers in Stockholm," Frank commented. "The whole city seems to be built on water."

"It is," Ilsa said. "In fact, Stockholm is made up of fourteen islands."

"Wow," Joe said. "I knew that Gamla Stan was an island."

"Norrmalm, where we are right now, is an island, too," Ilsa told them. "And if you look over that way"—she pointed to the west—"you'll see the island of Kungsholmen, which means King's Island."

Joe turned in the direction where Ilsa was pointing. A large building sat on the other side of a thin channel of water, with a red tower on top of it that dominated the skyline.

"What's that building?" he asked.

"That's the Stockholm City Hall," Ilsa said. "It's one of our most famous tourist attractions. You can see it from practically anywhere in the city. See those three golden crowns on top of the tower? That's the official symbol of Stockholm."

"Oh, yeah," Frank said. "I saw pictures of it at the airport and in the lobby of our hotel."

Ilsa led them along the docks and pointed out several tourist attractions visible above the surrounding buildings. She also indicated a small antiques shop that she told them belonged to one of Phoenix's clients, a man named Karl Bremer.

Suddenly Frank poked Joe in the ribs. Without speaking he nodded over his shoulder behind them. Joe pretended to tie his shoe so he could turn to see a familiar figure following about a block behind them—Agent Fairchild.

Ilsa led the Hardys up a hilly narrow street toward the center of the Norrmalm district. After they'd gone about a block, Ilsa spotted somebody she knew and paused for a moment to chat with her.

Joe turned to Frank. "Think we can ditch Fairchild?"

"It won't be easy with Ilsa along," Frank said. "But we don't want him to know that we're investigating Phoenix—even though he's probably guessed already."

Joe checked to see if the customs agent was following them, but Fairchild wasn't in view yet.

Suddenly there was the sound of an engine being gunned. Joe glanced around to see if he could locate the source.

A car pulled out of a parking space halfway down the hill accelerating rapidly, and it veered onto the sidewalk.

Astonished, Joe realized that it was heading straight for him and Frank!

Chapter

6

"WATCH IT!" Joe shouted to his brother. Frank and Joe both dived into the street. The car sped directly beside them, squealing as the driver tried to swerve in time to hit one of the Hardys. He didn't succeed.

The car continued past the brothers, and the few other pedestrians ran screaming to avoid being hit. The driver bumped off the sidewalk, turned down a side street, and vanished as quickly as he had arrived.

"Joe!" Ilsa shouted. "Frank! Are you all right?"

Joe stumbled back to his feet, wiping grime from his clothing. "Yes, I think so," he said. "You okay, Frank?"

"For the moment," Frank said, walking to his brother's side. "But it looks like somebody doesn't want me to stay that way."

"I can't believe that car actually tried to hit you!" Ilsa said. "Stay here and I'll see if somebody got the license number."

Ilsa ran over to the closest pedestrians and spoke to them in Swedish.

"I got a look at the driver when that car went past," Frank told him. "It was the same guy who tried to kill me in the maze last night."

"Oh, great," Joe said. "Obviously, somebody's serious about knocking us off. But why?"

"I don't know," Frank said. "It may mean we're getting close to something. That's a good sign. You know, I'm starting to wonder about your friend Ilsa."

"Huh?" Joe said. "What do you mean?"

"I was watching her when she was talking to her friend. She was facing down the hill—in the direction the car came from."

"So?" Joe said.

"So why didn't she warn us?" Frank asked. "She could at least have let us know we were about to get run down."

Joe's face turned pale. "That's a good question. I'm sure she must have an explanation, though."

"I'm afraid no one got the number," Ilsa said when she had finished talking with the other pedestrians. "The car vanished too quickly and everyone was busy getting out of its way."

"That's not your fault," Frank said. "But I was wondering why you didn't help us out back there. You know, yell out when you saw the car heading toward us or something."

Ilsa blushed and appeared embarrassed. "I'm sorry," she said. "I was too frightened. I tried to open my mouth to warn you, but I couldn't speak. I guess I was just—just stunned! Believe me, I could never have forgiven myself if something had happened to you."

Frank studied Ilsa's face carefully. There was no indication that she was lying, but it was impossible to be sure. Joe seemed convinced that she was telling the truth.

"I told you she'd have an explanation," he said with apparent relief.

The group walked for another few blocks until they came to another small warehouse district on yet another river. The Phoenix warehouse, Frank observed, was in an old redbrick building. Ilsa led them to a large loading platform that opened out onto the docks and into a large room bustling with workers carting boxes around.

Frank saw Ilsa's father, Jumsai Lee Khoo, emerge from behind a large stack of crates with a clipboard in his hand. He nodded his head in greeting at the Hardys and Ilsa.

"Good to see you boys," he said. "Ilsa told me that you'd be here this morning. I've wanted to see you, Frank. I heard about how you overcame the man who attacked you in Eleonora's garden yesterday. It would appear that you have some karate skills.''

"A few," Frank acknowledged. "Joe and I both studied martial arts back home."

"I am a student of martial arts myself," Khoo told him. "Ever since I was a child in Thailand, I have worked to improve my skills. I would be much pleased if you would visit my dojo before you leave Stockholm. It is at my home, not far from where Eleonora lives."

"And perhaps Joe and Frank can share dinner with us as well," Ilsa suggested.

"Agreed," Khoo said. "Just let us know when you have a free evening. I would be honored by your presence. Now, if you have any questions about Phoenix Enterprises, please feel free to ask."

"Well," Frank said, "what exactly does Phoenix do?"

"We're an import-export firm," Khoo explained. "We have a number of regular clients whose materials we ship to and from various destinations in Europe and Asia." He waved at the large piles of boxes in the warehouse. "You can see many of those materials here now."

"Are these some of the materials that Phoenix is importing?" Frank asked, pointing to the large pile of crates that Khoo had been inspecting when they arrived.

"Yes," Khoo said, though he made no attempt to tell Frank what the boxes contained. "It's a special shipment. Now, if we could just move on, I'll show you some of the other shipments that we'll be moving out of the warehouse today."

Khoo walked away, expecting the brothers to follow, but Frank took a moment to scan the boxes. Most bore a diamond-shaped logo with the name Diamond Systems emblazoned across it. A couple had the names of U.S. military bases.

"Isn't that Rutger Linska's firm?" Frank asked Ilsa.

"Oh, yes," Ilsa said. "We do a lot of work with Mr. Linska. He's a close friend of Ms. Grunewald's, after all. Of course, we work with a number of other inventors and corporations in Stockholm, even with some of the local military bases."

Khoo gave his daughter a surprisingly sharp look. "Now, now, Ilsa," he said with an edge to his voice. "I'm sure that your friends are not interested in all our business connections. We don't want to bore them with such details, do we?"

Go ahead and bore us, Frank thought, wondering why Khoo was so anxious to change the subject.

"I'm sorry," she told her father. "You're absolutely right."

"Does Phoenix import animals?" Joe asked. "I'm just curious because of all those animal rights people we saw outside Ms. Grunewald's estate last night."

"Yes, we do," Khoo said. "But I wouldn't believe everything that you hear from those animal-rights activists. We are quite conscientious in our animal-related activities. We never ship any animal without proper legal authorization. And we absolutely refuse to ship exotic birds or any animals that aren't properly and comfortably secured. Now, if you'll excuse me, I'm afraid I have further business to attend to."

"Well, where to now?" Frank asked Ilsa once Mr. Khoo had left.

"Surely you've seen enough of this warehouse," Ilsa said. "It really isn't very interesting."

Frank started to object, but it was clear that neither Ilsa nor her father wanted the Hardys to stay any longer.

"Okay," Frank said finally. "I'm looking forward to touring the city. How about you, Joe?"

"You bet," Joe said. Frank suspected, from the way his brother was smiling at Ilsa, that he was looking forward to a few more hours in her company—and probably wouldn't notice any sights but her.

As it turned out, Ilsa was equally preoccupied with Joe. She took the brothers to the National

Art Museum, where Frank was particularly impressed by a series of Rembrandt self-portraits.

"These are great," Frank said. "I remember seeing some Rembrandts when I was a kid and wishing I could draw like he did."

"Well, I know I don't have any artistic talent," Joe said.

"Oh, Joe," Ilsa said. "I'm sure you have a lot of hidden artistic talent."

"You think so?" Joe said.

"Hey, what about me?" Frank said, teasing them.

"Hmm?" Ilsa said, as though just noticing that Frank was still there. "Oh, I'm sure you have talent, too." She then refocused on Joe.

Frank began to feel like a fifth wheel as Ilsa's conversation was increasingly directed toward his brother. Finally he excused himself and left Ilsa and Joe to continue alone, telling them he had to go back to the hotel. Neither of them seemed to mind that he was leaving.

Joe barely noticed that his brother was gone. When they left the National Art Museum, at about one in the afternoon, Ilsa suggested that they head south across the bridge into Skeppsholmen, an island just to the east of Gamla Stan. It was a beautiful, sunny afternoon, and there were a large number of people crossing the bridge with them, oblivious to the cars racing past.

The island of Skeppsholmen was even smaller than Gamla Stan. Water was visible from just about any point on the island. Ilsa led Joe to one of the many docks surrounding Skeppsholmen. Joe was startled to see that there was a genuine three-masted schooner moored at the dock.

"That's some boat!" Joe said. "Are we allowed to go on board that thing?"

"Of course," Ilsa said. "That's why I brought you here. This is the AF *Chapman,* one of Stockholm's most famous attractions."

Ilsa led Joe up the plank and onto the wooden deck of the ship. Joe was surprised to see that the ship was filled with young people about the same age as Ilsa and himself.

"So what is this place?" asked Joe. "Some kind of museum?"

"No!" Ilsa laughed. "It's a hotel. A youth hostel, actually. Young people come from all over to stay here for a week or two while visiting Stockholm."

"Wow," Joe said. "If Frank and I had known about this place, we would have stayed here instead of in Gamla Stan."

"You might not have been able to get a room," Ilsa told him. "The AF *Chapman* is often booked for months in advance, especially during the tourist season, though it's sometimes possible to get a bed at the last minute if someone cancels. There are no individual rooms, just dormitories, separate ones for men and women."

Joe looked around at the wooden cabins and the many doors and windows that led into them. "This place is big for a sailing ship," he said. "I bet you could get lost on it."

"I bet you're right," Ilsa said. She smiled at Joe, a twinkle in her eye. Suddenly she darted toward the doorway.

"Ilsa," Joe began, "I'm not really sure—"

It was too late. She had already vanished. Joe ran toward the room where he thought Ilsa had gone.

Once his eyes adjusted to the shadows, he realized that he was peering into a room crammed with beds. A young man glanced up at him and said, "Can I help you?"

"I was just looking for a young woman," he said. "I think she went in here."

"This is a men's dormitory," the man said. "You'll have to look for your lady friend in the women's dormitory."

Joe stepped back out onto the deck and looked around. Where could she be? he thought to himself. He wandered to the rear of the ship, but there was no one there, least of all Ilsa. He leaned over the stern railing and craned his head to see if he could catch a glimpse of her back on the dock.

Suddenly there were footsteps behind him. Before Joe could turn he felt a heavy object crack the top of his head. Pain radiated through his skull like bolts of lightning. Joe was stunned by the sudden attack. His entire body folded beneath him, and he collapsed against the railing.

Strong hands grasped him from behind. Joe muttered a weak protest, but his attacker lifted him above the railing and tossed his limp body off the ship's stern into the water below!

Chapter

7

THOUGH ONLY HALF CONSCIOUS, Joe was aware that he was falling toward the water forty feet below the AF *Chapman*'s stern. He struck the water so hard that for a moment he was almost knocked fully unconscious. For about thirty seconds he sank like a stone toward the bottom of the river.

Snap out of it! whispered a desperate voice in Joe's head. If you don't do something, you're going to drown!

Sluggish and still only half awake, Joe began to paddle back up toward the surface of the river. Just as his lungs were aching to take in another breath he burst into the air, gasping desperately. From the dock he could hear voices crying out in Swedish.

There were several splashing noises as people jumped into the river to rescue Joe. Moments later he felt someone grab him by the shoulders and pull him toward the dock. Then several helping hands reached down and pulled Joe back onto dry land. By the time he lay gasping on the dock Joe was fully awake. He thanked his rescuer, a teenager with a stubbly blond beard and a deep tan.

"Joe!" cried Ilsa, racing across the dock from the direction of the AF *Chapman*. "What happened? Are you all right?"

Joe saw Ilsa staring down at him, concerned. He stood up and shook the water from his clothes.

"Yeah," he told her. "I guess I just got clumsy. I slipped and fell off the rear of the ship."

He knew it wasn't true, of course, but he watched Ilsa's face carefully as he said it, to see if she gave any indication that she knew he was lying. For a moment he thought he saw her brow wrinkle with doubt, but then she smiled.

"Let's get you back to your hotel," she said. "I think a cab is in order, even though it's costly."

It was hard for Joe to argue with that logic. His feet squished as he followed Ilsa to find a cab.

Frank, meanwhile, was searching for Agent Fairchild. Remembering what the agent had told them at the airport, Frank caught the bus to the

U.S. Embassy and asked for Fairchild at the front desk. He was directed to a small office, where Fairchild was seated behind a cluttered desk.

"Well, look who's here," Fairchild said sarcastically. "I've been looking for you kids all over Stockholm, and all I had to do was wait here for you to show up."

"We're all on the same side," Frank said. "I just wanted to find out how the investigation into the Kenya incident is going."

"And why should I tell you anything about it?" asked Fairchild.

"Because Joe and I are involved," Frank said. "Our father was killed in Mombasa. We'd just like to know how the investigation into his death is proceeding."

"We'll let you know as soon as we have some solid facts," Fairchild said, without offering any further information.

"Well," Frank said, "if *you* don't want to talk about it, why don't you call Ethan Daly in New York? Joe and I were working for him in Kenya and he might be willing to share some information with us."

Daly was assistant commissioner of U.S. Customs. It was Daly who had sent the Hardys to Kenya in the first place, though he had done so only at the urging of Congressman Kevin Alladyce, a client of their father's.

"It's only eight-thirty in the morning back in

New York," Fairchild said. "Daly might not even be at his desk yet."

"Why not give him a call?" Frank said. "Let me talk to him. We'll see if he's willing to share any information with me."

Reluctantly Fairchild picked up the phone on his desk and called New York. Minutes later he passed the receiver to Frank. Commissioner Daly was on the other end.

"Mr. Daly?" Frank said. "This is Frank Hardy. I'm in Stockholm."

"So I hear," Daly said. "I don't approve of you boys leaving Mombasa. I assume Agent Fairchild has told you that."

"Yes, he has," said Frank. "I just hoped that you'd be able to tell me how things are going in Kenya."

"As well as can be expected," Daly told him.

"What does that mean?" Frank asked.

"It means that that's all I'm going to tell you," Daly said. "You know that your mother is expected in Nairobi soon, don't you?"

"Your agents will look after her there, won't they?" Frank said.

"Someone will have to," Daly said pointedly. "You and your brother won't be there to help."

Frank quickly changed the subject. "Listen, I thought I should tell you that I was attacked last night, at a party in Sigtuna."

"What?" Daly exclaimed. "Why didn't you report this immediately?"

64

"I didn't have a chance," Frank said. "The man who attacked me was carrying a rather expensive and sophisticated-looking automatic pistol. It didn't look like the sort of thing an ordinary mugger would be using." Neither did the laser scope that had nearly ended Joe's life the day before, though Frank didn't mention that incident.

"That's very interesting," Daly said. Fairchild, too, seemed engrossed in what Frank had to say. In fact, Frank noticed that the agent glanced quickly down at a report sitting on his desk.

"If anything else like this happens, I want you to get in touch with Agent Fairchild immediately," Daly said. "Furthermore, I want you and your brother to back off from the investigation of Phoenix Enterprises. This is official business. Is that understood?"

"Yes, sir," Frank said. "That's understood."

He handed the phone back to agent Fairchild, who spoke briefly with Daly before hanging up. The customs agent turned and was about to ask Frank to leave when a staff assistant from the embassy walked through the door with a tray of coffee. As Fairchild rose to take a cup Frank jostled his elbow.

"Whoops!" Frank exclaimed as coffee sloshed onto the floor. "That was clumsy of me!"

"It certainly was," Fairchild said. "I'll get

some towels from the restroom. That stuff will stain the floor even worse than it is already.''

As Fairchild and the staff assistant disappeared into the hallway, Frank leaned over the agent's desk and glanced at the report that was sitting there. There was nothing about Phoenix Enterprises on the first page of the report, but there was something about an ''antiterrorist strike force.'' Clipped to the first page was a photo of a noted terrorist.

It was the same man who had attacked Frank at the party and had tried to run Frank and Joe down a few hours before!

''Are you still here?'' Fairchild reappeared in the door of his office. Frank stood up quickly, pretending to examine an ornate ashtray on the edge of the desk.

Fairchild unrolled a strip of paper towels and crouched in the middle of the floor to sop up the spilled coffee. ''If I were you, I'd go back to your hotel and make plans to head back to Kenya as soon as possible. Got it?''

''Got it,'' Frank said, heading for the door of the office. ''I hope my brother and I don't have to bother you again.''

Once outside, Frank hailed a cab and headed back to the hotel in Gamla Stan. On the way he thought long and hard about the picture that he'd seen on Fairchild's desk. There was no question that the man whose picture had been clipped to the report was the same man who had twice tried to kill him and his brother. Could this man work for Phoenix Enterprises?

If so, there was only one possible conclusion: Phoenix Enterprises was also involved with terrorists!

What was the connection, though? Perhaps Joe could help figure it out. He'd have to go back to the hotel and wait for his brother to get back from his "tour" with Ilsa Khoo.

Frank was surprised that Joe was already waiting in the hotel room. He was lying in the middle of his brass bed, pensively gazing at the ceiling.

"So what happened to Ilsa?" Frank asked. "I thought you two would be wandering around Stockholm for a couple more hours."

"We would have been," Joe said unhappily, "except that I ended up taking an unexpected swim in the river."

Joe told him the story. "I came back here so I could change my clothes," he concluded. "Ilsa wanted us to continue, but I sent her off from the lobby. I needed time to think."

"So do you believe Ilsa was responsible for getting you dunked in the river?" Frank asked.

"No," Joe said. "I mean, I don't know. That's what I've got to think about. I don't believe she'd do something like that, do you?"

"Well, *I* believe she'd do something like that!" snapped Frank. "And I think you're getting too close to Ilsa to realize it!"

"What?" snapped Joe in return. "Are you suggesting I'm letting my feelings for Ilsa stand in the way of finding Dad's killers?''

"That's exactly what I'm suggesting!" Frank said. "Ilsa's the daughter of one of the people who owns Phoenix. Don't forget that!"

"Just because Ilsa's father runs Phoenix doesn't mean she's part of the smuggling operation," Joe said.

"No," Frank said, "but it puts her in a pretty good position. Don't forget that!"

Joe shook his head. "I'm sorry. This is really getting to me. A girl I like may be trying to kill me. I need time to think this out."

Frank calmed down. "All right, I guess I understand. But there are a few more things you ought to know before you do any more thinking." He told Joe about the report on terrorism that he'd seen on Fairchild's desk and the picture of the man who'd tried to kill them.

"Who can we talk to who might know something about terrorists?" Joe asked.

"Mike Ryan," Frank said. "He's writing a series on arms smuggling, remember? I bet he's learned a thing or two about terrorist operations."

"Good idea," Joe said. "Let's give him a call."

The brothers called Mike, and he agreed to tell them what he knew about terrorists. He was busy for the next couple of hours, but he arranged to meet them early that evening at his apartment.

To kill time while waiting to see Mike, Frank and Joe left the hotel and walked south through Gamla Stan. They ended up in a large public square with benches where people were sitting and talking and feeding birds.

Joe spotted a plaque with the name Stortorget Square written on it in Swedish. To one side of the square was a large structure with a sign identifying it as the Borsen Building.

"I've heard of that," Frank said. "It's where the Swedish Academy meets. They oversee the Nobel Prize for literature."

After wandering around the square for another hour, the brothers caught a bus to Mike Ryan's apartment. He was standing in front of the building when they arrived. As soon as they stepped off the bus, he led them toward a small side street where his car was parked.

"We'll grab dinner in Norrmalm," Mike said as they walked. "I've got a lot to catch you guys up on. But I'm only telling you all of this because you're already involved in this Phoenix affair. Some of this information could be dangerous to you if anybody finds out you know it."

"I think we can handle it," Frank said.

"First of all," Mike said, "Phoenix is in deep trouble with the World Society for Animal Protection. That's the animal-rights group that was picketing Eleonora Grunewald's place last night.

69

It seems that despite Phoenix's claim to the contrary, the society has proof that Phoenix has been shipping animals under cruel conditions. They plan to take Phoenix to court over it if possible. The society may also have been responsible for hijacking some of Phoenix's shipments, but nobody really knows for sure.

"I also know the big arms deal I mentioned last night is going down sometime in the next two or three days," Mike continued. "I don't know exactly when or where, but there are a lot of big-time terrorists involved. I've also heard rumors that there's some kind of connection with the U.S. military, but I don't know exactly what. I'll be investigating that rumor this evening, after I finish talking to you guys."

"The U.S. military?" Joe said. "This is getting more and more mysterious."

They were at Mike's car, and he reached out to grab the door handle on the driver's side. Abruptly he jerked his hand back.

"Ow!" he exclaimed. He held his hand up and opened the palm. There was a red slash across the middle of it, with blood running down toward his wrist.

"What happened?" Joe said. "You're bleeding!"

"I don't . . ." Mike started to say, then he began swaying. "Something's wrong. . . ."

Suddenly his knees buckled, and he collapsed

in the street. Frank and Joe grabbed him by the shoulders and tried to help him back to the sidewalk.

Mike peered up at Frank. "Hidden . . . prize. . . ." he gasped. Then his eyes rolled up in his head, and he fell into unconsciousness.

Chapter

8

"MIKE!" Joe said urgently. Frank held his hand in front of Mike's nose—he was still breathing. A car honked at the brothers to get out of the street. Struggling against Mike's bulk, they managed to haul him onto the sidewalk.

"We need to call an ambulance!" Joe said.

Frank ran to a nearby phone booth and called the emergency number printed on a label at the top of the telephone casing. Although the operator at the other end spoke little English, Frank managed to get her to understand that they needed an ambulance in a hurry.

While they waited for the ambulance to arrive Joe checked the door of Mike's car. A small razor blade was hidden underneath the handle.

"That's a standard assassin's technique," Frank said when Joe told him about it. "Put poison on the blade and leave it where somebody will get cut on it. Which is more evidence that we're up against trained terrorists."

Joe stared down at Mike Ryan's limp body. "What was it that Mike said right before he passed out?"

"Something about a 'hidden prize,'" said Frank. "I have no idea what it means."

The ambulance arrived within five minutes and took Mike and the Hardys to a hospital in Norrmalm. At the emergency room a white-coated doctor with a neatly trimmed brown beard asked the Hardys to sit in the waiting room until he could check on Mike's condition. An hour later the doctor reappeared, quite concerned.

"How's Mike?" Frank asked. "Is he going to be okay?"

"That's difficult to say," the doctor told him. "We've identified the poison that was used on him, and there's no effective antidote for it. We can only offer him symptomatic treatment and hope that his body will be able to fight back."

"You mean that he could die?" Joe asked.

"I'd say there's a very good chance of it," the doctor said reluctantly. "In fact, I don't think there's more than a ten percent chance that he'll recover. I wish I could offer you better news than that, but I can't."

"When will we know for sure?" Frank asked.

"Perhaps within the next forty-eight hours or so," the doctor said. "If he holds on that long, I'd give him a fighting chance."

"Well, we know that Mike's a fighter," Frank said.

"Yeah, like our father!" snapped Joe miserably.

"I'm afraid that you're going to have to speak with the authorities," the doctor said, nodding toward a police officer at the door. "They're going to want to know exactly what happened to your friend."

The doctor waved the officer into the room, then left. The officer began to ask tough questions about Mike's "accident," but the Hardys pretended to know nothing about how it happened.

"We were going out to dinner," Frank said. "Mike was in the middle of telling a joke when he reached out to open his car door."

"The last thing he said was 'ouch,' " Joe reported, "and then he collapsed."

"Are you sure you know nothing else?" the officer asked. "I find it hard to believe that you have no suspicions at all about what happened to your friend."

"Take my word for it," said a familiar voice. "They don't know anything about it."

The brothers turned to see Agent Fairchild

holding up his identification for the police officer to look at.

"I'm from the U.S. Embassy," Fairchild told the police officer. "I'll take over from here."

"As you wish," the officer said, tipping his hat to the customs agent.

"How did you find us?" Joe asked.

"The American authorities have friends in the Stockholm police," he said. "They let us know whenever an American is in trouble."

"And you came to help us out," Frank said sarcastically. "That's really nice of you."

"I thought I asked you kids to get out of Stockholm and head back to Kenya," Fairchild said, ignoring Frank's comments. "Next thing I know, I get a report that you're involved with a mysterious murder attempt. Can't you kids stay out of trouble for half a day?"

"I guess we're just having a run of bad luck," Joe said.

"Yeah, sure," Fairchild said. "It was my bad luck to get assigned to baby-sit you kids in the first place. I want you to go straight back to your hotel room, do you hear me? And I don't want you to leave it except to go to the airport and leave this country."

"We're on our way," Frank said as he and his brother headed toward the emergency room exit. "But we're not leaving until we hear whether Mike Ryan is okay."

"Or until we find out who murdered our father,'' whispered Joe, in a voice too low for Fairchild to hear.

In the lobby of their hotel the young desk clerk called out to the Hardys as they walked past.

"There were two telephone calls for you," he said, handing them a pair of message slips. One of the messages was from Ilsa; the other was from the Hardys' mother, who had left a return number in Nairobi.

Back in their room Joe called Ilsa. She wanted to see Joe the next afternoon. Joe told her he'd see her if he had a chance.

Joe then studied the message slip from his mother. He turned and looked at Frank.

"What should we tell her?" he asked.

"Nothing," Frank said. "There's nothing we can tell her. But I guess we'd better call her back. I just wish I knew what to say."

Joe wandered to the window of the hotel room, lost in thought. He knew that his mother was probably more devastated by the loss of their father than he and Frank were, and he wished that they could be by her side. But he also felt a driving need to find his father's killers, and his mother was not likely to understand that.

He stared out into the Stockholm evening, still almost light as day. Shoppers were walking up and down the sidewalk looking for antique stores that were still open.

He also saw two large men in leather jackets staring up at their hotel window. Their faces were grim and unsmiling.

"Frank?" Joe said. "Come take a look at this."

As Frank made it to the window the men stepped off the curb and walked rapidly toward the hotel.

"What is it?" Frank asked.

"There were a couple of guys across the street watching our room," Joe said. "I think they're on their way over here now."

"Do we want to be here when they arrive?" Frank asked.

"I don't think so," Joe said. "They appeared to be large and unfriendly."

"Then let's get out of here," Frank said. He opened the door to the hall and peered outside.

The sound of heavy footsteps rang out from the nearby stairwell. "Uh-oh," Frank said. "I think they're on their way up already."

He stepped back into the room, closing and locking the door. "Maybe if we wait in here quietly, they'll go away."

"I'm not so sure about that," Joe said, "but I guess we don't have much choice."

Joe listened as the door at the top of the stairwell opened and the footsteps proceeded into the hallway. The footsteps grew louder until they came to an abrupt halt—directly outside the Hardys' room!

There was a brief silence followed by a clicking sound. Joe recognized it immediately as the sound of a gun bolt being cocked.

Frank turned to Joe urgently. He mouthed the words "We'd better hide."

Where? Joe shrugged broadly, indicating that there was no place in the small room where they could conceal themselves. Surely the strangers would think to check under the beds and inside the closet.

Suddenly Frank had an idea. He pointed toward the window, which was half open. Directly outside the window was a ledge that extended along the entire front of the building.

A squeaking sound came from the doorway as someone tested the door handle. Frank pushed the window gently upward, then crawled out onto the ledge. Joe followed.

The ledge was about fifteen inches wide. As Joe crawled through the window and crouched on the narrow stone surface he glanced cautiously down at the street below.

The Hardys' room was at least seventy feet above the street. Joe swallowed hard, then forced himself not to look down. He hesitated for a moment before pulling himself all the way through the window, but a sudden banging sound on the door of the hotel room gave him all the motivation he needed to go the rest of the way.

Frank was already standing on the ledge, his

back flattened against the side of the building. Joe climbed to his feet and shuffled his way to his brother's side.

"This way." Frank led Joe toward the corner of the building, where an ornate Roman column stood.

"I don't see any way down, but I think we can make it up to the roof." Frank pointed to an elaborate filigreed design in the stonework where the column met the roof. Frank reached up to the stonework and gripped an overhanging portion of the filigree and pulled himself up. A few seconds later he was on the roof. Joe grabbed the stonework and pulled himself up after his brother.

Just then from the open window of their hotel room came a loud shattering noise, as though someone had just battered open their door. Joe peered over the edge of the roof to see a shadowy figure lean out of the window they had just exited.

"We'd better get out of here before they figure out where we've gone," Joe told his brother.

Frank pointed toward a door that opened onto the flat rooftop and apparently led to a flight of stairs. "That looks like the exit—" Suddenly they heard the sound of footsteps echoing up the stairs, heading for the roof.

"Too late!" Joe cried. "They're already on the way up!"

"Where do we go now?" Frank said. "That's the only way off the roof!"

Joe looked desperately toward the roof of the next building. There was no time to measure how far away it was from the roof on which they were standing, but it could have been anywhere from five to fifteen feet.

Frank and Joe exchanged glances. Could they make it to the other roof in a single jump? The sound of pounding footsteps from the stairwell behind them told them that they had no choice. Moving as one, they raced toward the edge of the roof—and leapt into space!

Chapter
9

IF WE DON'T make this jump, we'll be dead! Frank thought to himself as he and Joe flew across the gap between the two buildings.

He hit the roof with a loud *thwack!* as his brother landed at almost the same instant. He collided with the hard shingled surface of the roof, and the crack of bullets sounded from the roof behind him. Frank heard the whistle of a bullet pass inches above his head!

Unfortunately, the roof on which Frank and Joe had landed was not flat. Rather, it was slanted, and Frank immediately found himself sliding down it. Two more bullets struck the shingles just above his hands, sending fragments of roof spraying across his face. Before his adversary could fire again Frank tightened his grip on the shingles and pulled himself up and over the gabled roof of the building with Joe following.

Huddled on the other side of the roof, the brothers were safe—for the moment. But even as Frank was catching his breath he heard a loud thump on the other side of the roof, followed by a second thump.

"Those guys are here already," he said to Joe.

"Let's go!" Joe cried.

The angled roof on which they were sitting led down to an ornately carved gutter about ten feet below. The brothers slid down the shingled surface until their feet caught on the gutter, then they made the short jump across to the next roof. Frank turned and saw two dark figures clambering their way over the peaked roof on which they had just been. At the sight of the Hardys the two figures scrambled down to the gutter in pursuit.

The roof of the next building was flat and slate covered, but there was no staircase leading into the building below. The Hardys raced across that roof and paused on the other side, searching for a way down.

A narrow drainpipe plunged from the edge of the roof to the ground far below.

"Think we can climb down it?" Frank asked.

Joe studied the next roof, which was at least twenty feet away. Definitely too far to jump.

Then he glanced back at the pursuing figures, who had just jumped onto the roof on which they were standing.

"Either that or we'd better figure out a way to make ourselves bulletproof," Joe said. "Start climbing!"

Frank grabbed the drainpipe and shimmied his way down it as fast as he could. It wasn't easy to keep a grip on the pipe, but the sides were rough enough so that he could keep himself from falling off if he moved fast and used his feet to slow his descent on the brick sides of the building. Joe started down after him just as the sounds of more gunshots rang out from above.

Frank raised his eyes for a moment and saw that the two thugs were sliding down the drainpipe, too. Good thing they need both hands to hold on, Frank thought to himself.

Frank jumped the last five feet to the pavement. Seconds later Joe was standing next to him. They were in a wide but deserted alley lined with trash cans and piles of old newspapers. One end of the alley was blocked by a fence. At the other end they could see the river that ran to the east of Gamla Stan.

"We're blocked by the river!" Frank shouted as Joe raced down the alley behind him.

"I hope these guys can't swim," Joe replied, gasping for breath.

"I hope we don't have to swim," Frank said, pointing to a small pier at the end of the alley.

Joe scouted the pier and saw a single outboard-motorboat moored to it. "Let's go for it!" Joe shouted.

The Hardys jumped on board the tiny boat. Joe untied the line that secured the boat to the pier, and Frank yanked the starter. The motor roared to life, and the boat leapt away from the pier, almost colliding with a small buoy floating a few feet offshore.

Frank checked back over his shoulder to see the two men who had been pursuing them race onto the pier. They fired at the Hardys, but the bullets disappeared harmlessly into the water.

"They'll never catch us now!" Joe shouted.

"Don't push your luck," Frank said. "We haven't gotten away yet."

"Hey, what can they do?" Joe asked. "We've got a boat, and they don't. They'll never catch us."

At that moment another motorboat zoomed past the Hardys and headed toward the pier. As it slowed down and approached a mooring post one of the gunmen jumped on board, slugged the driver, and tossed him into the water. The other gunman jumped in after him. Within seconds the gunmen were once again racing in pursuit of the Hardys.

"Maybe I did speak too soon," Joe said. "Can this thing go any faster?"

Frank cranked a handle on the motor. "We'll find out," he said.

At Frank's urging the tiny motorboat lurched forward, but the motorboat being piloted by the gunmen had no trouble keeping up with them. In fact, Frank noted, it was gaining on them slightly.

"Go around that way!" Joe shouted, waving his hands to indicate that Frank should head north around the tip of the island off Skeppsholmen.

"That's where I'm headed," Frank said. "I just hope I can stay in front of those guys long enough to make it around the next bend!"

Frank looked back at the other boat. One of the gunmen was steering while the other tried to draw a bead on the Hardys, but the vibrations from the motor caused his hand to shake so badly he wasn't able to get off a shot.

Finally Frank whipped the boat around the eastern side of Skeppsholmen. For a moment the gunmen in the other boat disappeared, their view blocked by the island itself.

Joe waved at a network of wooden docks. "Go over there, fast, before they come around the bend!"

Frank steered the boat in among several large yachts and cut the motor. Then he and Joe flattened themselves against the bottom of the boat.

The gunmen sped past the docks without noticing the Hardys. Finally Joe peered over the edge of the boat.

"It's safe," he said. "Let's get out of here

before they figure out what happened and come back.''

"I hope the guy who owns this boat can find it over here," he said. He pulled a bill out of his pocket and tucked it under one of the seats.

"What's that for?" Joe asked.

"Gas money," Frank said. "I don't want anybody to say we don't pay our bills."

"How do you suppose those guys knew about our hotel room?" Frank asked as the brothers walked shakily back to dry land. "Mike was the only person who knew where we were staying, and I know he wouldn't have told anyone."

Frank stopped walking. "Wait a minute!" he said. "Ilsa also knew where we were staying."

"What's that supposed to mean?" Joe asked angrily. "Are you implying that Ilsa set us up?"

"That's exactly what I'm implying," Frank said. "Who else could it have been? You'll notice we weren't attacked at the hotel until after Ilsa took you back to your room."

"Maybe somebody followed us," Joe snapped. "And Mike's not the only one who knows where we're staying. Agent Fairchild knows, too."

"Oh, I suppose you think those two thugs were sent to get us by U.S. Customs?" Frank said. "Get real, Joe!"

"Maybe Fairchild was working with Jellicoe," Joe said. "Did you think of that?"

Frank sagged with exhaustion. "I don't know what I think," he said. "I'm too tired to think."

"Yeah," Joe said. "I think I'm too tired to get back to our hotel room." He nodded toward the AF *Chapman,* which was only a block from where they were standing. "But I think I know a closer place where we can sleep."

The two brothers boarded the AF *Chapman* a few minutes later and asked if any beds were available. The bearded man outside the men's dormitory told him that there were not, but when Frank produced a few kronor from his pocket the man suggested that he might be able to find space for the Hardys. They wound up sleeping on a pair of small cots in the back of a room filled with young male travelers from all over Europe. By this time, however, the brothers were too exhausted to notice the cramped accommodations or to carry on a conversation with any of their new companions. Within minutes both Frank and Joe had fallen into a sound and dreamless sleep.

The reception that they received the next morning at their own hotel was far less friendly than the reception at the AF *Chapman.* As Joe pushed open the front door and walked into the lobby the desk clerk emerged from behind the counter and blocked his path.

"You!" shouted the young red-faced man. "It's about time you showed up! That must have been quite a party you held in your room last night!"

"Party?" Joe asked. "What party?"

"Don't pretend to be innocent," the clerk snapped. "We found your room in a mess this morning. The door was open, the lock broken, and your belongings tossed all over!"

Frank groaned. "I think I see what happened. Listen, we're very sorry, and we'll pay for the damage. It won't happen again."

"I should think not," said the clerk, though he seemed somewhat more satisfied when Frank handed him a stack of kronor. "We run a respectable establishment here."

His anger diminished, the desk clerk pulled a message slip from behind the counter and handed it to Joe. "You had another phone call while you were gone," he said.

Joe studied the slip. "It's from Congressman Alladyce, back in the States," he said. "He wants to thank us for finding out what happened to his friend Chris Lincoln in Kenya."

"Well, it's nice to know he hasn't forgotten us," Frank said. "I guess Daly must have told him where we are staying."

The boys wondered again if they should have returned to their hotel, but they decided no one would think they'd return there, so they'd be safe. They hoped they had figured it right.

Inside their room Joe glanced around at the

mess. Their bags had been opened, and their clothes and other belongings were strewn about. Nothing seemed to be missing, however.

"Guess those two guys came back for another look around," Frank said. "I don't think they found anything, though."

"Maybe they just wanted to make a mess," Joe suggested. "Get revenge after we made fools of them."

Joe shrugged and went down the hall to take a shower. While he was gone Frank reached under the chest of drawers and pulled out a small object he had taped to its underside. It was the gun he had found in the maze. It was practically the only solid clue they had to the identity of their father's murderers, and he was glad the two thugs hadn't found it. Fortunately the gunmen hadn't felt on the bottom board under the chest when they'd ransacked the room. Pulling a piece of rope from his suitcase, Frank strapped the gun to his ankle, then pulled his pants leg down over it. He was reluctant to show the gun to Joe, perhaps because his brother would think he was crazy to lug it around with him.

After resting a couple of hours the brothers decided to pay a visit to the hospital where they had left Mike Ryan the night before. They headed back to the main avenue that ran through the middle of Gamla Stan. Seeing an automobile rental agency, they decided to rent a small car instead of hailing a cab. Given the cost of cabs in Stockholm, it turned out to be only slightly more expensive.

The brothers then drove to the hospital. The nurse at the reception desk told them that Mike was still in his room on the fifth floor but had not yet regained consciousness and was not allowed visitors.

"Well," said Joe as they walked away from the desk, "should we just leave without seeing Mike?"

"No," Frank said, veering toward a staircase. "I think we should go upstairs on our own. I'm sure no one would mind."

On the fifth floor they headed for the room where Mike was staying. At the far end of the corridor they could see an orderly pushing a lunch cart into Mike's room.

"Wait a minute," Joe said. "If Mike's unconscious, why are they bringing him lunch?"

As though he had heard them coming, the orderly turned toward the Hardys. Frank recognized him immediately. It was the man who had tried to kill him in the maze!

"That's no orderly!" cried Frank. "That's our friendly neighborhood terrorist!"

Frank and Joe sprinted down the hallway. The terrorist shoved the lunch cart in their direction and bolted through the door into Mike's room.

Nearly colliding with a nurse coming out of

another room, Frank shoved the lunch cart aside and shouldered Mike's door open.

Even as he burst inside Frank saw that the killer had the window next to Mike's bed open and was starting to push Mike's limp body over the sill!

Chapter

10

"HEY, YOU!" shouted Frank, sprinting across the room toward the assassin.

The killer turned to him briefly, then continued pushing Mike's upper body through the window. Frank realized that he intended to drop the reporter to his death five stories below!

Frank grabbed Mike's ankles and pulled him back inside. The killer started shoving Mike's shoulders back out the window, so Frank was relieved when Joe helped him with Mike's legs. The killer realized he was overmatched and fled for the door of the room. Joe blocked his way, which unfortunately left only Frank to support the dangling Mike and keep him from tumbling out the window. Gravity and momentum worked against Frank, and Mike began sliding toward the street below. Only his feet remained anchored in the window.

The killer's fist lashed out at Joe's chin, but Joe neatly sidestepped the blow and grabbed the man by the collar. Before Joe could wrestle his opponent into submission, however, the killer brought his knee up and caught Joe in the stomach, giving him a chance to make another rush for the door.

"Oof!" grunted Joe, staggering backward from the blow as the assassin raced out the door and down the hallway.

"Hurry, give me a hand!" cried Frank, straining to keep Mike from falling all the way to the ground.

Wincing with pain, Joe staggered to the window and took one of Mike's legs from Frank. Together the brothers pulled him back into the room.

"What are you doing?" cried a nurse from the door of the room.

"I think your patient's taking a turn for the worse," Joe said as he helped Frank pull Mike back onto the bed. "You'd better get a doctor in here fast!"

Joe was relieved to hear the doctor say that Mike's condition was unchanged, despite his near plunge from the window. Before the Hardys left the hospital room Joe looked up and saw Agent Fairchild in the doorway—with the Stockholm police right behind him. This time Fairchild didn't chase the police away but allowed them to question the brothers in a conference room on the ground floor.

"I find it difficult to believe that you know nothing about why these people want to kill Mike Ryan," the police officer said to Frank. It was the same officer who had questioned them in the emergency room the day before. "Surely he must have told you something that would indicate why his life is in danger."

"Why would he tell us?" Frank asked. "Mike's just an old friend of the family, that's all. He isn't going to let us in on any secrets."

"Besides," Joe said, "if he knows something that's all that dangerous, why would he want us to know it, too? Then our lives would be in danger."

The Stockholm police officer seemed to be half convinced by this explanation, but Agent Fairchild was dubious.

"Somehow I get the feeling you kids aren't leveling with us," he said. "I'd guess you know more than you're telling—a lot more."

"Okay," Joe said, pulling Fairchild aside so the police officer couldn't hear. "Mike said he was working on a story about arms smuggling. Maybe the people who are trying to kill him have something to do with illegal arms sales. Satisfied?"

"That's better," Agent Fairchild said. "But how does this connect with Phoenix Enterprises? I know you kids have been snooping around the Phoenix offices. I saw you walking around with Jumsai Khoo's daughter yesterday."

"Who says the arms sale has anything to do with Phoenix?" Frank said. "You can't expect us to tie all your loose ends together. Mike was working on this story before we arrived."

Fairchild sighed. He asked the brothers a few more questions and then let them go back to Mike's room. He never mentioned their leaving Stockholm again. He must have known his threats were futile.

"Fairchild's right," Joe said once they were alone in the room with the unconscious reporter. "There must be a connection between Phoenix and this arms deal that Mike is writing about. Why else would the same guy who tried to kill us try to kill Mike?"

Frank sagged against the wall of the hospital room. "I don't know," he said mournfully. "I wish I knew what to think."

"Let's get going," Joe said. "We're not doing Mike—or Dad—any good by just standing around."

When they arrived back at their rental car Frank said, "I think we should pay a visit to Rutger Linska. I definitely consider him a suspect in this case. Especially after that conversation I overheard between him and Eleonora Grunewald.''

They drove to the address that Linska had given Frank, which turned out to be a low brown building on the edge of town. A woman at the front desk rang Linska's number, then directed the Hardys down a hallway to a room in the back. There were uniformed guards at both ends of the hallway, and they regarded the Hardys with suspicion.

Linska's laboratory was narrow and cluttered, with desks covered with blueprints and at least five computer terminals, two of which were displaying color animations of missiles in flight. Linska looked up from one of the screens and smiled at his visitors.

"Frank!" he said, extending his hand in greeting. "It's good to see you! I had hoped you would take me up on my offer for a tour of my lab.''

"Well, we had some free time, so we thought we'd stop by,'' Frank told him. He introduced Linska to Joe, who had been so absorbed in his conversation with Ilsa on the night of the party that he had never been introduced to the engineer.

"So,'' said Joe, "Frank told me you work with missiles. Do you keep the prototypes around here?''

"I'm afraid not,'' Linska said with a shrug. "Those are manufactured elsewhere. Here we do mostly brain work. I use these computers to design the systems, then pass on the blueprints to the factory.''

Frank pointed at the computer where Linska had just been sitting. The video display showed a full three-dimensional animation of a missile zeroing in on a large building.

''That looks almost like a video game,'' Frank said. ''Is that really an accurate representation of a missile?''

''Oh, yes,'' Linska explained. ''These are extremely accurate simulations. I told you the other night that I work on guidance systems based on artificial intelligence algorithms. All my work can be done on the computer. Then the software can be recorded on a disk and moved to the actual missile.''

Frank watched Linska as he talked. Although he had seemed nervous and ill at ease at Eleonora Grunewald's party, the engineer seemed perfectly confident and at home surrounded by his computers and blueprints. He was almost a different man.

''It's amazing what we can do with computers,'' Linska was saying. ''I can sit at my desk and fight an entire war just inside my machine. By the time I've finished testing my software on this computer I know how it will behave in any situation. I almost don't need to build the missile itself.''

''But don't you feel a little funny about designing weapons of war?'' Joe asked. "Do we really need better weapons, better missile guidance systems?''

An odd expression crossed Linska's face. "There will always be war,'' he said. "And the wars of the future will be nothing like the wars of the past. They will be quick, decisive, over almost as quickly as''—he gestured toward the animation that was still proceeding on the screen of the computer—"as a video game.''

Frank shuddered. This Rutger Linska really was different from the one he had met at the party! On the outside he was still the quiet little nerd, but he talked like a villain from a futuristic spy thriller. Frank almost regretted having to change the subject.

"Er, I was wondering what your connection is with Phoenix, Rutger,'' Frank asked. "I know that you and Eleonora Grunewald are good friends. Does Phoenix import the hardware that you need, or are you actually doing some sort of contract work for them?''

Linska's reaction to Frank was sharp, as though he was irritated at having his train of thought broken. "My connection with Phoenix is nothing important,'' he said dismissively. "Ms. Grunewald has done a few favors for me, and I for her. That's all.''

Joe walked over to some boxes lined up against the wall. "I noticed these boxes have the Phoenix label on them,'' he said, pointing out the circle with a large birdlike creature pictured inside it. "And this one here"—he stepped closer to one of the boxes—"has the address of a U.S. military base in Iceland."

Linska descended angrily on Joe. "Please step away from those boxes," he said quickly. "They contain delicate equipment. You could damage them merely by standing too close to them!"

He guided Joe back to the middle of the room, then turned to Frank. "I'm afraid you've picked a rather bad time to visit," he said. "I'm in the middle of some very important work. Perhaps we could meet again later."

"Uh, right, Rutger," Frank said, grabbing his brother by the arm. "Come on, Joe, I think it's time to grab some lunch."

Outside the laboratory Joe looked back at the building and scowled. "Boy, he changed moods in a hurry, didn't he?"

"He sure did," agreed Frank. "He didn't like to talk about Phoenix at all. Or about those boxes. What do you suppose was bothering him?"

"I don't know," Joe said. "But I'd like to find out."

They left Linska's office and climbed into their rented car.

"I think I'll give Ilsa a call," Joe said as he drove back into town.

"I can't believe you, Joe!" Frank exclaimed.

"What's the matter?" Joe asked. "Do you still think Ilsa's involved with the bad guys?"

"I think maybe you're a little too interested in chasing after girls and not interested enough in finding the person who killed our father!" snapped Frank in return.

Joe's face flushed a bright red. "You don't have any right to say that! What I feel about Ilsa isn't any of your business!"

Frank pulled the car over to the side of the road and parked. He glared at Joe angrily. "I think I have a right to comment on how you're handling this case. And I think your involvement with Ilsa is starting to get in the way!"

"Well, if you think that," shouted Joe, "why don't you just go looking for Dad's killer on your own? See how you do without my help!"

"Maybe I'll do just that," yelled Frank, popping open the door to the car and storming out. They were parked near a wide stone bridge with carved statues at the entrance. Frank slammed the door and stormed down a small hill leading to the river below.

He had made it halfway there when he heard a sound overhead like the whine of a small jet or missile. Frank raised his head to identify the source of the noise but saw nothing.

Thinking it must have been his imagination, he started to turn away. Just then there was a shattering explosion, and Frank saw the rented car in which his brother had been sitting explode in a bright ball of orange flame!

Chapter
11

"JOE!" FRANK YELLED, rushing back up the hill to the burning car. He tried to get close enough to the car to open the door, but the heat of the flames drove him away.

"No!" he screamed angrily, furious at himself for leaving Joe in the car alone. First his father had died while he watched, and now the same thing had happened to his brother!

Suddenly he became aware of someone at his side. He turned to find Joe observing the smoldering ruins of the car.

"Where'd you come from?" Frank asked in astonishment. "I thought you were in the car!"

"Huh-uh," said Joe, his voice tempered by shock. "I got out of the car to go after you and got knocked to the ground when it exploded. A couple of seconds earlier and I *would* have been in the car.''

''Are you okay?'' Frank asked.

''Yeah,'' Joe said. ''I'm just a little—a little dazed.''

''Let's get out of here,'' Frank said. ''I saw a small park at the bottom of the hill, in the shadow of the bridge.''

Frank took his stunned brother by the shoulder and helped him down the hill. When they reached the park Joe sat on a bench and stared at Frank numbly.

''I'm sorry, Frank,'' Joe said. ''About what happened back in the car. I shouldn't have gotten angry with you.''

''No,'' Frank said, sitting next to Joe. ''I'm the one who should apologize. These last few days have been incredibly tough for both of us. First Dad, then Mike. It's been too much for us.''

''I'm just so confused,'' Joe said. ''I like Ilsa, but you're right, I don't know whose side she's on in all of this. She might even be one of the people who killed Dad.''

Frank leaned back against the bench. ''This has got to be the toughest case we've ever tackled. I'm not sure yet where it's all leading. In the beginning it seemed pretty simple. Somebody was smuggling animals. But now there seem to be terrorists and who knows what else involved as well.''

"So," Joe said, slinging an arm across his brother's shoulder. "Where do we go next?"

Frank cracked an unexpected smile. "I've got an idea." He reached into his pocket and pulled out a small golden-colored key. "I took this from Mike's pocket last night before the ambulance arrived. It's the key to his apartment. We can check out his word processor to see what he's been writing about.''

"Good work, big brother!" Joe said. "Now, if we can only figure what we're going to tell the rental agency about their car . . ."

An hour later the Hardys climbed out of a cab in front of Mike Ryan's building. Once inside his apartment Frank turned on the computer and sat down at Mike's desk.

He tapped a few keys and read the words that appeared on the display. "Mike uses the same word processing program that we do. This ought to make things easier.''

Frank typed a command and waited for the word processor to finish booting up. Then he called up a list of files. Bright green letters appeared on the computer screen, listing all the word processing files that Mike had stored on his hard drive. There were several dozens of them. Frank ran his fingers down the list, checking for one that might have anything to do with arms smuggling.

"Here's one called ARMNOTES.TXT," he told his brother. "Think that's it?"

"Can't hurt to take a peek," Joe said.

Frank loaded the file. After reading the first paragraph he knew that he had called up the correct file.

"This is the one," he said. "There's a lot of stuff here about black market weapons." He began reading the contents of the file to Joe. It took about half an hour to read, and by the time they were done the brothers had received a short lesson in the illegal arms trade.

"It seems," Frank said as he skimmed the files, "that weapons have been vanishing—from warehouses of private arms dealers and U.S. military bases around the world. Sometimes these weapons get lost as the result of documented thefts, sometimes they just vanish."

"Vanish?" asked Joe.

"Into thin air," Frank said. "It seems as if Mike made contact with some people involved in the illegal arms trade, and they talked with him on the condition that their names not be used in any article that he wrote. He only refers to them by cryptic initials."

"What did these people tell him?" Joe asked.

"They told him that someone out there is buying a lot of arms," Frank said. "In some cases they arranged for those arms to be stolen from military bases and other storehouses. In other cases they bribed officials to route arms shipments to them and erased the records from all computers. Some of these stolen arms have already shown up on black market auction blocks. Others haven't surfaced yet."

"What kind of arms are we talking about?" Joe asked. "Pistols? Machine guns? Missiles?"

Frank scanned forward through the file. "Apparently all types, from guns like the one that guy tried to kill me with the other night to missiles like the ones that Rutger Linska is designing."

"Or like whatever hit our car this afternoon?" Joe suggested.

Frank thought about it for a second. "Yeah, like that," he said. "There's something here about hand-held antipersonnel launchers. That sounds like what somebody probably used to take out our car."

"Whew!" said Joe. "It sounds like a lot of nasty artillery may be falling into the wrong hands!"

"It sure does," Frank said. "Hey, here's a list of the places that the arms have been stolen from." He scanned down the list, then turned to Joe. "You'd better take a look at this!"

Joe looked over Frank's shoulder. "Hey, those are the names of the U.S. military bases that we saw written on the boxes in Rutger Linska's lab and at the Phoenix warehouse!'' Joe exclaimed.

"Do you think we've found a connection between Phoenix and the terrorists?" Joe asked.

"Those stolen and missing weapons could have ended up in Rutger's lab and in Phoenix's warehouse," Frank concluded.

"And don't forget what Mike said about the big arms deal that was about to go down in the next day or two," Joe said.

"Which means that a lot of black market arms may be going on sale to the highest bidder within the next twenty-four hours, if nobody does anything about it," Frank said.

"And with Mike out of commission," Joe said, "we may be the only ones who can do anything about stopping it."

Joe sat down on Mike's sofa. "I think," he said, "that it may be time for us to ask somebody for help. This is too big for the two of us."

"Agreed," Frank said, "but who can we turn to? Is there anybody we can really trust?"

"What about Fairchild?" asked Joe.

"I'm not sure about him," Frank said. "We trusted U.S. Customs once before, and look where it got us. Jellicoe betrayed us, and Dad ended up getting killed."

"True," Joe said. "Maybe we should tough this out on our own a little longer. But what do we know about this arms operation? Does Mike say anything in that file about where this sale is going to take place?"

"No," Frank said. "He never mentions the arms deal in his notes. Maybe that's something that he considered too hot to put into the computer."

"Well, then, what do we know about Phoenix?" Joe asked. "Maybe some of the people we've met over the last couple of days are involved with the arms deal."

"How about Eleonora Grunewald?" Frank suggested. "She just got back from Mombasa, which makes her a prime candidate in my book."

"And she's a friend of Rutger Linska's," Joe said. "Remember what you overheard him telling Ms. Grunewald about a shipment? That could refer to the arms deal itself."

"True," Frank said. "Maybe Linska is her expert on armaments. Eleonora Grunewald could be using Phoenix as a cover for smuggling operations—both arms smuggling and animal smuggling."

"I don't know who to trust anymore," Joe said.

Frank thought about it for a minute. "Maybe there is somebody we can trust," he said.

"Who?" Joe asked.

"That animal-rights organization that Mike mentioned," Frank said. "The World Society for Animal Protection."

Joe didn't understand. "We don't know anything about them. How do we know we can trust them?"

"We know they don't like Phoenix," Frank said, "which makes them okay in my book."

"Maybe you're right," Joe said. "All right, let's go talk to these animal-rights people."

The Stockholm offices of the World Society for Animal Protection were located in the center of Norrmalm, only about two miles from the Phoenix warehouse. Joe knocked on the door, which was opened by a slender woman in her late twenties wearing faded jeans and a T-shirt with a silhouette of a blue whale on the front.

"We'd like to talk with you about Phoenix Enterprises," Joe said.

"Are you from Phoenix?" she asked. "Or are you interested in helping us fight them?"

"Neither," Frank said. "Actually, we were hoping you could help us get some information on Phoenix."

The woman furrowed her brow. "I'm not quite sure I understand."

The Hardys explained how they had been involved in breaking up the animal-smuggling operation in Mombasa. As they told their story the woman's expression changed from disbelief to admiration.

"That's wonderful!" she said. "We've heard all about Mombasa here, but we hadn't any de-

108

tails. I'm sorry to hear about your father, though."

"Yeah," Joe said. "We think Phoenix was involved in his death, and that's why we came here to investigate them."

"We'll help you in any way possible," the woman said sincerely. She led them into a small, cluttered office lined with file cabinets. After browsing through one of the cabinets, she handed Frank a folder labeled Phoenix Photos.

"This may help," she said. "These are photos that we believe support our claims against Phoenix. Take a look and see if there's anything there you need."

Frank and Joe leafed through the stack of photos inside the folder. After a few minutes Joe cried out victoriously.

"Here!" he said. "This is the guy who tried to kill us and Mike! Recognize him?"

He passed the photo to Frank. "Uh-huh," Frank said. "Do you recognize the location?"

Joe studied the photo again. The familiar figure of the assassin was surrounded by uniformed workers carting boxes around a warehouse.

"The Phoenix warehouse!" Joe said.

"Bingo!" Frank agreed. "Here's another!"

Frank pulled a second photograph from the stack, this time showing the assassin standing in the middle of a public square surrounded by park benches.

"Stortorget Square," Joe said. "That's the Swedish Academy building in the background."

After a few more minutes they had two more pictures of the assassin, one that showed him standing on the docks near the warehouse and another that showed him on a street in Norrmalm.

"That street looks familiar," Joe said. "I think it's one of the places Ilsa took us the other day."

"Right," Frank said. "You see that antiques shop in the background? Ilsa said it belonged to one of Phoenix's clients."

"Oh, yeah," Joe said. "What was his name? Brunner? Brenner?"

"Bremer," Frank said. "Karl Bremer. The name stuck in my mind for some reason."

"Do you suppose we should investigate him, too?" Joe asked.

"Maybe," Frank said. "If we have time."

The Hardys thanked the woman and handed back the folder full of photos. They exited the society offices and stood for a moment on a street corner.

"What do we do now?" asked Frank. "We've got a few leads. Which do we follow first?"

"We're not far from the Phoenix warehouse. I think we should check that out first. The special shipment that Linska was talking about at the party may be there."

Joe agreed. The boys decided to get something

110

to eat first, then head for the warehouse. They ate at a small restaurant in Norrmalm, then walked the two miles to the Phoenix warehouse.

It was evening by the time they arrived, and all the workers should have been home. But the door to the loading dock was open. A large green truck covered with a khaki-colored canopy that gave it a military look was pulled up to the dock, and workers were moving crates into the back of it.

Standing on the dock directing these operations was an individual whom Frank recognized. "Eleonora Grunewald," he whispered to Joe as they stood in the shadow of a neighboring building.

"Well, she does work for Phoenix," Joe said, "so I'm not surprised to find her here."

"What do you suppose they're loading into that truck?" Frank asked. "Stolen weapons?"

"Could be," Joe said. "Maybe we should move in for a closer look."

It was too late. One of the workers pushed the back door of the truck closed, and the driver revved the engine. As the truck pulled away Eleonora Grunewald climbed down from the loading dock and slid into a small car. Frank heard her say something to one of the workers about going home, then she drove away after the truck. Another worker closed the door to the loading dock.

"So much for getting a closer look," Frank said. "Now what?"

"Let's follow Eleonora Grunewald and that truck," Joe said. "I bet they lead us straight to the big arms deal."

Frank had started to move out of the shadows to hail a cab when a pair of hands shot out from behind him and clamped around his mouth and shoulders. He tried to fight back, but whoever had grabbed him was too strong. There was a muffled cry from Joe, and then Frank found himself being carried helplessly into the alley next to the Phoenix warehouse!

Chapter

12

AS QUICKLY AS the hands had grasped him, Frank felt them let go. He spun around to face his attackers and found himself face-to-face with a pair of hulking Stockholm police officers. Behind them stood an angry Agent Fairchild. Next to him were a couple of men in suits who Frank suspected were special agents from U.S. Customs.

"You two kids don't give up, do you?" Fairchild said. "We've had the Phoenix warehouse staked out all day, hoping to nail them on animal smuggling charges, and you boys almost messed everything up for us. We've already got agents tailing that phony military truck. We don't need a couple of loose cannons rolling around on the deck, too. Especially a pair of amateur loose cannons.'' He pronounced the word *amateur* as though it left a bad taste in his mouth.

Frank and Joe exchanged curious looks. Fairchild hadn't said anything about terrorists or the arms deal. Frank wondered if he was covering up or simply refusing to take them into his confidence. Or was it possible that he actually knew nothing about the arms deal?

"Then I guess you don't need us around," Joe said. "So we'll just go back to our hotel.''

"Not so fast," Fairchild said. "I've had enough of you kids. I'm going to see to it that you're shipped back to Kenya on the next flight out so you can't cause any more trouble.''

"Thanks," Frank said, "but no thanks. I think we can book our own flight back to Kenya.''

"I bet you can," Fairchild said. "And I bet you won't." He turned to the police officers. "Lock them in the back of the surveillance van.''

The officers escorted the Hardys to the far end of the alley where a large police van was parked. One of the officers opened the rear door, motioned the Hardys inside, and closed the door behind them.

Frank and Joe listened as the lock on the door clicked shut. They looked around the interior of the van.

It was dimly lit by a small light bulb behind a

wire frame on the ceiling. In the middle of the van sat a laptop computer console atop a small table. At the opposite end from the door was a bank of communications equipment, beyond which was a metal gate blocking off the rear portion of the van from the driver's compartment. The gate was held shut by a large padlock.

Joe examined both ends of the van and sighed. "No way out," he said. "Looks like Fairchild is serious this time."

"I'm not so sure about that," Frank said, sitting on a small hassock someone had placed next to the communications equipment. "I'd feel better if he were really playing serious."

"What do you mean?" Joe asked.

"I mean there's no way to be sure that he's serious about tracking down the smugglers inside Phoenix," Frank said. "And even if he is, how do we know he's chasing after the right person? He's trailing Eleonora Grunewald now, but what if Grunewald isn't the one behind the arms deal?"

"Well," Joe said, "that conversation between her and Linska sounded pretty suspicious."

"True," Frank said, "but she still doesn't strike me as the sort of person who would be responsible for this kind of operation."

"So Fairchild's off on a wild-goose chase?" Joe asked.

"Could be," Frank said. "And while he's off

chasing Grunewald, you and I are locked in the back of this van doing nothing.''

Joe smiled. "Then I guess we'd better get out of this van. Do you have your lock-picking tools with you?"

"I never leave home without 'em," Frank said. He pulled what looked to be a fat fountain pen out of his pants pocket. Unscrewing one end of it, he removed several slender metal tools. Then he slipped around to one side of the bank of communications equipment and started working on the padlock that held the metal gate closed.

After about two minutes of work the padlock was open. Frank pulled it away from the latch and slid the gate open.

"You want to drive, or shall I?" Frank asked his brother.

"I'll do it," Joe said, sliding past his brother and into the driver's seat of the van. "You fool around with that computer and see if you can turn up anything interesting."

Frank settled down in front of the laptop and turned it on. Meanwhile his brother found a set of keys under the floor mat, stuck one in the ignition, and revved the engine. There was the sound of shouting from the rear of the van, but before anyone had a chance to catch up with them Joe had steered the van out of the alley and into the streets of Stockholm.

"Where should I go?" shouted Joe.

"I don't know," Frank said. "Just drive around a little while I check to see what's in this computer. Maybe I'll be able to find a destination for us."

"Better hurry up," Joe said. "Within a few minutes every cop in the city will be out looking for this van!"

"Oh, I don't think we're that important," Frank replied. "It'll probably only be every other cop."

The computer's internal disk drive was filled with data files about the Phoenix case. Frank called up a file entitled GRUNEWALD.DAT and scanned it. As he suspected from the file name, it was all about Eleonora Grunewald. According to the file, she was the mastermind behind Phoenix's smuggling operations. The evidence against her included a number of phony documents relating to the smuggled merchandise—documents that bore her signature. And she had recently returned from Mombasa in the company of a suspected terrorist named Abdul Deharr.

Frank wasn't surprised that the description of Deharr sounded exactly like that of the man who had repeatedly tried to kill them.

So, thought Frank, did this mean that he was wrong about Eleonora Grunewald? Could she be the mastermind behind the Phoenix smuggling operation after all?

Somehow it didn't fit. Frank's instincts told

him that the police were on a wild-goose chase. If so, it was up to him and Joe to put them back on the right path.

But what was the right path? Frank hoped that the answer lay somewhere in the police computer sitting in front of him.

He called up a second file called CLIENTS.DAT. It was a list of Phoenix clients, some of them Swedish. He called out a few of the names to Joe, but none of them gave the Hardys any new information.

"You know what I've been thinking about?" Joe said as he steered the van around a block full of large buildings. "That picture we saw at the World Society for Animal Protection offices of that Abdul in front of the Swedish Academy building. What was he doing there? And what was the name of that building again?" Joe asked. "The one where the Swedish Academy meets?"

"Huh?" said Frank, who was staring at a list of Swedish names on the computer screen. "It was Borsen, I think."

"Oh, yeah," Joe said. "That's right."

Frank felt a sudden rush of excitement. "Borsen!" he exclaimed. "That's it!"

"That's what?" asked Joe.

"Remember that word I saw in Chris Lincoln's notebook?" Frank asked. *"Orsenb?* I thought it was probably some Swahili word. After all, Lincoln was an American agent working in Kenya. It never occurred to me that it might be a Swedish word! It's just a slightly scrambled version of Borsen!"

"Okay," Joe said. "So where does that get us?"

"I don't know," Frank said, "but it must get us somewhere."

"Wait a minute," Joe said. "What was that thing that Mike said just before he became unconscious?"

"Something about a 'hidden prize,' " Frank said. "I still haven't figured out what that means."

"I don't think he meant that to be a complete sentence," Joe suggested. "Maybe he was trying to say that something was hidden, like the missing weapons. Prize might mean a Nobel prize. Something might be hidden at a Nobel *prize* building."

Frank turned to his brother, astonished. "That's just crazy enough to be true," Frank said. "I hope you've got this van headed toward Gamla Stan, because I think it's time we checked out the Borsen Building."

"I'm on my way," Joe told him.

Ten minutes later Joe parked the van on a secluded side street next to Stortorget Square in the middle of Gamla Stan. He and Frank climbed out, walked to the square, and peered up at the Borsen Building.

Joe scanned the area. "I don't see any sign of

that truck we saw at the warehouse," he said. "If this is where they're putting the stolen weapons, I doubt that they've had time to get here and unpack them already."

"Maybe they haven't arrived yet," Frank suggested.

"Then they must have taken a really long route," Joe said. "Or gotten a flat tire."

The area around the building was deserted. Frank and Joe moved closer until they were in a shadowed area next to the entrance.

"So how do we get inside?" Joe asked. "Just walk through the front door?"

Frank pointed at a small window just above ground level. Through the window he could see a basement room.

"We can hope that this is unlocked," Frank said. "I'd hate to have to break the glass to get in."

"Yeah," Joe said. "I'm running out of kronor to pay for all the damage we leave behind."

Frank slipped his fingers around the edge of the window pane. Slowly he pulled it open.

"Looks like a tight squeeze," he said, "but I think I can get inside."

Frank slid his feet through the window first. Seconds later he landed on the stone floor of a small, dusty room. Joe slid in after him.

The room was deserted. An old bed against one wall looked as if it hadn't been slept in for some time.

"Looks like an old janitor's quarters," Frank said. "Probably nobody uses it anymore."

Joe opened the door to the next room. A dimly lit hall led past several doors. At the far end was a stairway and another hall heading off at an angle from the first.

"Come on," Joe said. "Let's take a look down there."

He led the way down the hall. The floor was dusty, but where the second hall joined the stairway they saw footprints in the dust.

"Looks like somebody's been down here recently," Joe said.

"It's not time to give out the prize yet," Frank said, "so maybe our friends from Phoenix were here."

"Maybe," Joe said. "Let's see where they went."

The Hardys followed the footprints down the adjoining hall. They continued past several doors and came to an abrupt halt at the far end of the hall—at a blank wall!

Frank peered at the wall curiously. Why would footprints lead up to a wall and just stop?

"There ought to be a door here," he said.

"Maybe there is," Joe said. He reached out and pushed against the wall—

The wall swung backward as though it were on a hinge. Joe looked at Frank with wide eyes.

"A secret door!" Joe said.

"We haven't seen one of these in, oh, several months," Frank said.

Joe stepped through the door, followed by Frank. The room inside was pitch black, no windows. Joe reached around in the darkness until his fingers touched a string dangling from the ceiling. He pulled on it, and a light switched on.

Frank and Joe gasped simultaneously. The room was only moderately large, but it was filled with equipment.

And not just any equipment: weapons. All kinds of weapons. Pistols, rifles, machine guns, even hand-held missile launchers.

Enough weapons to fight a small war!

Chapter
13

"I THINK WE'VE HIT the jackpot," Frank said.

"Are there any small countries you'd like to take over?" Joe asked.

Many of the weapons were still inside crates. Joe began looking at the crates one by one. Some were marked with the Phoenix emblem, others with the names of foreign military bases. Rutger Linska's diamond-shaped logo was on several of the boxes, as were the symbols of other companies that were affiliated with Phoenix Enterprises.

"Be careful," Frank said, pointing to the pile of crates that Joe was examining. It was stacked almost to the ceiling and was starting to lean precariously toward the center of the room.

"That pile looks pretty heavy. You don't want it falling on top of you."

"I'll be careful," Joe said. "I don't want to damage any of this merchandise before the authorities get a look at it."

A sound from the hall caused Joe to turn around. Footsteps were pounding rapidly down the stairway!

"Somebody's on the way!" Joe cried. "Hide behind those boxes!"

"Right," Frank said. He looked around and found a small opening behind two large crates and crouched in it. Meanwhile Joe pushed the secret door closed, then turned off the small ceiling lamp. Blindly he stumbled after Frank and crouched behind the crates.

Moments later the secret door opened and the light flashed on again. Joe listened as heavy footsteps crossed the floor only a few feet from where he was hiding. It sounded to Joe as though there were two men in the room with them, though whether they were in the room to deliver more weapons or carry away some of the old ones, he couldn't tell.

"I'll be glad to have this thing over with," one of the voices said in heavily accented English. If the boys had to speak only one language, English was the best.

"Agreed," said a second voice with a slightly different accent. "In a few more hours the sale will be over. That will be a relief. Maybe we can find some time to relax.''

"What about Sigtuna?" the first voice asked. "Who's taking care of that?"

"Our two friends are up there," the second man said. "They know what to do. There'll be no more trouble from Sigtuna after tonight."

Joe leaned forward, trying to hear more. Suddenly the box behind which he was hiding was pulled away, and he found himself staring into the face of a large man with a scar and a dark mustache.

"Where'd you come from?" the man snarled. "Get out of there!"

He grabbed Joe and pulled him into the center of the room. The other man, who was taller than the first and had long, stringy blond hair, spotted Frank and grabbed him, too.

"Spying on us, eh?" said the blond man. "How did you two kids get in here?"

"You've been eavesdropping on us, haven't you?" the second man asked. "What did you hear?"

"Eavesdropping?" Frank said. "I don't know what you're talking about."

"Yeah," Joe said. "We were just looking around the building here and stumbled into this room. We hid behind those boxes because we thought we'd get in trouble."

"Well, you are in trouble," the blond man said. "A lot of trouble."

"So what are we going to do with these kids?" the man with the mustache asked his companion. "We can't let them go. They've heard too much."

"We'll have to dispose of them," the blond man said, "the same way we always do. Feed them to the fish at the bottom of the Saltsjon River."

The man with the mustache grabbed Joe and started to pull him toward the door of the small room. At the same time Frank reached out and shoved the precariously piled boxes that Joe had been examining moments before.

The stack of boxes instantly started falling toward the center of the room! Frank hopped nimbly aside, and Joe dived out of the way of a falling crate, but the two men could only raise their eyes in horror as the boxes plummeted toward them.

"What the—" screamed the blond-haired man, his words cut short as a heavy box struck him in the face. His companion flailed backward as he tried unsuccessfully to catch a heavy crate. Within seconds both men had nearly vanished under the rain of boxes.

Joe vaulted over the pile of equipment. "Good work!" he shouted. "That should hold them for a while!"

"It only has to hold them for a few minutes," Frank said, racing back into the hall. "Let's get out of here!"

He and Joe headed back to the small room where they had entered and crawled back through the window. Then they hurried across Stortorget Square to the street where they had left the police van.

They climbed into the rear of the van. Frank threw a switch on the bank of communications gear and turned a dial on one of the radios.

"We can probably use this to radio the authorities," he said as staticky voices came out of the speakers.

"I'll drive while you take care of that," Joe said, crawling back into the driver's seat. "Where should we go?"

"Sigtuna. That's where Eleonora Grunewald lives," Frank said. "You heard what those guys said about their friends 'taking care of business' in Sigtuna. That sounded pretty sinister to me. I have a feeling that something funny may be going on there. And I've been wanting to get a look inside that mansion of hers since we were at the party the other night."

Joe started the van and headed north. Frank turned on the small transmitter in the back of the van, grabbed a microphone, and began broadcasting.

"Attention!" he announced. "This is Frank Hardy. My brother, Joe, and I are driving a borrowed police van to Sigtuna, to visit the estate of Eleonora Grunewald. If you want your van back, I'd suggest you meet us there."

He then added some information about the secret room in the basement of the Borsen Building and hung the microphone back in its rack. If that didn't get them help from the police, nothing would!

A half hour later Joe pulled the van up to the gates of the Grunewald estate. The guards who had been standing watch the night of the party were gone, and the gates stood open. Pausing for only a second, Joe gunned the engine and continued up the hill to the small parking lot next to the mansion.

He parked the van, and the Hardys climbed out. The mansion seemed deserted.

"Guess Ms. Grunewald isn't throwing any parties tonight," Joe said. "Should we see if anybody's home?"

"Yes," Frank said, "but let's not knock on the front door. If somebody is home, I'm not sure it's a good idea to let them know we're here."

Frank led Joe to a large window on the side of the house. Looking in, they saw a startling sight.

Eleonora Grunewald was struggling against two hulking male attackers—the same two men who had chased the Hardys in the motorboat! One of the men was holding a hypodermic needle and was about to plunge it into the helpless woman's arm!

Chapter

14

"LOOKS LIKE we got here just in time!" Joe said. He grabbed a large flagstone from the walkway that ran beneath the window and hurled it with all his strength through the glass.

The man with the hypodermic looked up, startled. The other man released his grip on Eleonora Grunewald and turned toward the window.

"Who is there?" he shouted.

Eleonora Grunewald took advantage of the distraction and yanked the arm of the man holding the needle. The hypodermic flew out of his hand and shattered against the wall behind her.

Frank Hardy jumped onto the windowsill and knocked the rest of the glass out of the window with his foot. Then he leapt into the room.

"Sorry to ruin your fun, guys," he announced. "But it didn't look like you were playing fair."

"Yeah," Joe said, leaping into the room after his brother. "Two big guys against one woman. We figured we'd help even the odds."

"You two!" snarled the man who had been holding the hypodermic. He was a tall bald man dressed in military fatigues.

"How convenient that you came to us," said the other man, who had curly red hair and a protruding jaw. "This will certainly save us a lot of trouble! We were going to look for you after dispatching Ms. Grunewald."

The bald-headed man advanced on Frank, a mocking grin on his face. "You gave us the slip the other night in the river," he said, "but now we'll see how you do in hand-to-hand combat!"

Frank desperately wondered if he and Joe hadn't been a little hasty about rushing into the room. As the man advanced on him, however, he crouched into a karate pose and lashed out at his attacker with one foot. The man stumbled backward, startled.

Suddenly there was a thudding noise, and the man's eyes rolled up in his head. He fell forward and sprawled on the floor. Behind him stood Eleonora Grunewald, a heavy vase in her hands.

The red-haired man spun around toward Ms. Grunewald. Before he could act, however, Joe leapt forward and tackled him around the waist, knocking him across the room and through an open door leading into an adjoining corridor.

"Gotcha!" cried Joe as the man's head thumped sharply against the wooden floor. With a groan the red-haired man's head slumped to one side, unconscious.

"Good thinking," Frank said to Eleonora Grunewald. "Those guys were just a little bigger than Joe and me. We needed the help."

Eleonora Grunewald slumped into a high-backed antique chair and began trembling. "I was so afraid," she said in a quavery voice. "If you two hadn't arrived, I'm not sure what I'd have done."

Frank and Joe found some rope and tightly bound the two unconscious men. Then they turned back to Eleonora Grunewald.

"What exactly was happening when we broke in?" Frank asked, stepping to her side. "It looked like that guy was going to give you a little unplanned medication, and I had a feeling he wasn't your doctor."

"No," Ms. Grunewald told him. "They were going to kill me, but they wanted to make it look like a suicide. They forced me to write a note saying that I had decided to take my own life, then they took a bottle of medicine that my doctor had left for me. They were going to inject it into me all at once."

"But why?" Joe asked. "What did you do to get them angry?"

"Let me guess," Frank said. "They wanted to make it look like you were behind Phoenix's smuggling operations, right?"

Eleonora Grunewald nodded her head in agreement. "Yes, yes. But it's all a lie." Tears welled up in her eyes. "I've been signing papers at the request of my partners, but I didn't realize the papers involved anything illegal. But I had begun to suspect that something was wrong. After a while I discovered that my partners were involved in the illegal smuggling of arms and animals, but I was too frightened to do anything about it."

"Which partners?" asked Frank.

"Jumsai Khoo and Lyle Banner," she told them. When Frank showed no recognition of the second name, she explained: "Banner is in charge of the American office. He's based in New York. He's always traveling, engaging in deals, and Khoo was in charge of operations at the warehouse. But I was the one who brought most of the military and scientific clients to Phoenix. Jumsai was involved with Middle Eastern and Asian clientele, Banner with U.S. clients. Khoo was so busy that he even had his daughter handling a share of his work. Paperwork, mostly. But I was the one who carried the main load."

"What about Rutger Linska?" Joe asked. "What did he have to do with all of this?"

"Rutger?" Ms. Grunewald said. "Poor dear

Rutger! He had nothing at all to do with it. He and his computers. He has no time to worry about such petty human pursuits as smuggling. He's too caught up with his machines.''

"What were you doing in Mombasa?" Frank asked. "Joe and I just came from there, where we were involved with breaking up Phoenix's poaching operations. When we heard you'd been there we assumed you must have been involved in illegal activities there.''

"No, no," Ms. Grunewald said. "My trip to Mombasa was supposed to be a vacation. It had nothing to do with smuggling or poaching. But then Ilsa called me and said that her father wanted me to meet with a man named Abdul Deharr, who he said was a potential client for the firm.''

Frank glanced at Joe. "I warned you that Ilsa was involved in this," he said.

"I don't believe it," Joe said defensively. "I want to ask her about this myself the next time I see her.''

"The next time you see her," Frank said, "she may be in jail.''

Joe stared at Frank angrily but didn't respond. Then he said, "Where are the security guards around here, anyway? This place was crawling with them the other night.''

"Why, I don't know," Ms. Grunewald said. "They should have been here by now. Those two men must have done something to them.

There's a guard booth not far from the main gate. You can call down there from one of the phones and check."

"Where's a phone?" Joe asked. "I don't see one in here."

"There's one down the hall," she told him. "Second room on the right."

"I'll be right back," Joe told Frank. "I'm going to call the guards."

Joe left the room and walked down the hall to the phone. The number of the guard booth was printed next to the dial. He called it, but there was no answer. Then he made a second call—to Ilsa.

Her phone rang twice before Ilsa answered. Joe's heart jumped at the sound of her voice.

"Ilsa?" Joe said. "Boy, it's good to hear your voice. I'm in Sigtuna. I've got to talk with you. It's really important. But not at your home."

"There's a church up the road from Eleonora's mansion. It's really an old abbey. You can't miss it."

Joe hung up the phone and raced out of the house to the police van. I have no time to explain to Frank, he thought, his heart pounding. I must see Ilsa!

Joe gunned the van through the main gate. A groggy guard stood up and waved his arms for Joe to stop.

"This is an emergency!" Joe shouted. "Tell my brother I've gone to the abbey up the road."

* * *

Meanwhile Eleonora Grunewald dabbed at her eyes with a handkerchief. "I want to thank you again for saving my life," she told Frank. "You really didn't need my help, you know. Those were impressive karate moves that you were making. I'd be willing to bet you could have taken care of that man all by yourself."

"Thanks," Frank said. "But I don't mind getting a little help."

"You know, Jumsai Khoo is into karate," she told him. "Under other circumstances you and Jumsai might have gotten along rather well."

"Yes, he complimented me on my karate skills, too," Frank said. Something clicked into place in Frank's head even as he spoke the words. How in the world had Khoo even known about Frank's karate skills? There had been no witnesses to the fight in the garden—except for the killer himself. How, then, did Khoo know that Frank had used karate against his attacker?

Unless it was Khoo who had sent the killer after him in the first place!

Frank rushed out of the room and into the hallway. "Joe!" he cried. He ran to the second room on the right and looked for his brother inside. There was no sign of him.

What had happened to Joe?

Frank raced to the front door and out to the parking lot. He looked for the van, but it was gone. Apparently his brother had vanished with it!

135

Angry, Frank raced down the hill to the guard booth that Eleonora Grunewald had mentioned. On the way he found two groggy guards heading up to the mansion.

"What happened?" Frank asked. The guard explained that they had been attacked by the same men who had assaulted Ms. Grunewald.

"Let's go back to the house," Frank told them. "Did you see my brother out here?"

"Uh, I believe so," said one of the guards groggily. "At least the fellow looked a lot like you. He said he was going to the abbey up the road."

Frank asked the guard for more details about the abbey, then led them both to the house, where he asked them to watch over the two killers that he and Joe had left tied up on Eleonora Grunewald's rug.

Finally Frank spoke briefly with Ms. Grunewald and asked if he could borrow her car.

Moments later Frank was speeding off down the driveway of the Grunewald estate—in Eleonora Grunewald's shiny new Jaguar.

Joe pulled up in front of the abbey where Ilsa had suggested they meet and parked the van on a level plot of grass. The abbey, a large stone structure, appeared to be several centuries old. Its walls were dark gray. High atop the abbey rose a bell tower.

The front door of the abbey was open. Joe

stepped inside and looked around for Ilsa. He found himself in a small chapel with large stained-glass windows. Sitting in one of the pews beneath a window was Ilsa, who appeared to be absorbed in thought. She raised her head abruptly at the sound of Joe's footsteps.

"Joe!" she said. Joe was thrilled that she was happy to see him but also a little concerned by the fear that he heard in her voice.

"I need to talk with you, Ilsa," he said. "It's about your father."

"My father?" she said. "I—I don't understand."

"Frank and I have reason to suspect that something has gone very wrong inside Phoenix," he told her. "And we think your father is involved."

"My father?" she said, appearing to be perplexed. "But why do you suspect him?"

"Frank and I have been attacked several times in the last few days," Joe said, "but never when you're close enough to us to get hurt. The guys who have attacked us have always waited until you weren't around. Like when that car almost ran us down. The guy who was driving it didn't try to hit us until you went off to talk with your friend. And whoever dunked me in the Saltsjon the other day waited until you were off playing hide-and-seek."

Ilsa shook her head. "What does that have to do with my father?"

"Don't you get it?" Joe said. "He wants Frank and me out of the way, but he doesn't want you hurt. So whenever we're with you, we're safe—temporarily."

"Very clever, Joe," said a voice from the shadows. Joe watched as Jumsai Khoo stepped toward him from the ornate altar at the front of the chapel. "You and your brother have been giving me no end of trouble."

Joe froze at the sound of Khoo's voice.

"I've been looking for you and Frank all evening. I'm glad that I've finally found one of you. The word is out that someone reported my little cache of weapons in the Borsen Building to the authorities—and that those same authorities are now coming after me. I'm afraid that some of my men will probably tell the authorities what they want to know, which will present a problem. You and Frank were responsible. Am I right in that assumption?"

"Father, what are you talking about?" Ilsa asked.

"Quiet, Ilsa," Khoo said. "I need to speak with Joe for a minute. I'll have a word with you later."

"You told me Joe wouldn't get hurt," Ilsa said.

"I won't hurt him," Khoo said. He was holding a coil of rope. "I'm only going to tie him up so that I'll have a chance to escape before the authorities arrive."

Khoo pulled a gun from his pocket and pointed it at Joe. Ilsa gasped as Khoo motioned Joe to follow him to the front of the chapel.

"I want to show you something, Joe," he said. "Have you ever been in the bell tower of one of these old abbeys? The view is absolutely magnificent."

"Um, I don't think I'm interested in seeing that, Mr. Khoo," Joe said. "I think I've had enough sightseeing for this visit."

"Oh, I wasn't suggesting that you take a look at the bell tower, Joe," Khoo told him. "I was ordering you to do so. And the one with the gun always gets to do the ordering."

"Makes sense," said Joe as Khoo prodded him toward a small staircase next to the altar.

"Up the stairs," Khoo told him. "Now!"

Joe entered the narrow doorway to the staircase. The stairs were old and winding and completely unlit. Joe stumbled forward into the darkness, making his way gradually up the shaft of the bell tower.

"If all you want to do is tie me up," Joe said, "why do you want me to go up to the top of the bell tower? So I'll have something to look at while I wait for the cops?"

"I just want you in an out-of-the-way place, Joe," Khoo said. "That's all."

Joe reached the top of the stairs and looked around. He was standing in a small room with large window-size openings on all four sides. In the middle of the room hung a gigantic iron bell.

Khoo stepped into the room behind Joe. "Please move over a little closer to the wall," Khoo ordered.

"Since you just plan to tie me up, I think I'll be comfortable there." Joe pointed toward the middle of the room.

"Sorry. I've changed my plans," Khoo said. "Please move over toward that opening."

Joe looked out and shuddered. They were at least a hundred feet above the ground.

Suddenly Khoo lunged at Joe, shoving him toward the window. Joe grabbed at Khoo's gun, but before he could get a grip on it, Khoo brought up a knee and caught Joe in the groin. Joe staggered backward.

"I apologize for the crudity of my methods," Khoo said, "but this is the end for you, Joe."

Khoo lunged at him again, but this time Joe kicked out and caught Khoo's gun arm with the toe of his shoe. With a grunt of pain Khoo let go of the gun, which flew out into space.

Unfortunately, the maneuver caused Joe to stagger toward the opening. Unable to get his balance, Joe found himself falling over the edge of the windowsill toward the ground a hundred feet below!

Chapter

JOE WOULD BE KILLED by his fall, he knew for certain! Unless he could do something to stop it.

Before he was completely out of the window Joe saw a large stone projecting outward just a foot below the opening. He threw his arms out desperately and was just able to wrap them around it before the momentum of his fall propelled him past it.

For all the good it would do him . . .

Joe was now dangling in space, his feet flailing helplessly in the air. Only the strength of his arms was preventing him from slipping the rest of the way to the ground—and his strength was quickly diminishing!

Joe looked up at Jumsai Khoo, who stood at the window above him, determination on his face.

"I'm afraid that won't help you," Khoo said as he stared down at Joe. "You can't dangle there forever."

Khoo began to lean out of the window. Then, from far below, Joe heard the sound of a car driving up to the abbey. Concern crossed Khoo's face, and he stepped back from the window.

"I'm afraid I must be going," Joe heard Khoo say. "I trust you won't be able to hang on for long."

Joe groaned. Khoo was right. There was no way he could pull himself back up to the bell tower without help, and his arms were starting to ache from the strain.

It was a long way to the ground below!

At the wheel of Eleonora Grunewald's Jaguar, Frank raced up the road to the abbey. On the way up the winding road, however, he was nearly run off it by a car coming the other way. Frank was unable to see who was in the vehicle and considered turning around and following it. But he decided he'd better check out the abbey first.

The place seemed to be deserted. There was no one in the small chapel, but Frank thought that he could hear a noise from the bell tower above.

He strained to listen. It was his brother's voice! Calling out for help!

Frank raced up the dark stairs to the bell tower to find his brother.

"Get the rope!" Joe called up.

Frank spotted the coil of rope on the floor. He picked it up, knotted one end of it, and tossed the knot to Joe.

Letting go with one hand, Joe grabbed the knot, then wrapped his second hand around it.

Frank pulled with all his strength, and slowly Joe made his way back into the tower.

"What happened?" Frank asked.

"It was Khoo," Joe explained. "He's the one who's been trying to kill us. When he heard you driving up he got scared and took off. He must have driven off with Ilsa just before you got here."

"So that's who was in that car," Frank said. "Yeah, I also figured that it must be Khoo trying to kill us. Since he's involved with arms smuggling, he's probably responsible for trying to kill Mike, too."

"Come on," Joe said. "Maybe we can still catch them!"

The Hardys raced back down the stairs and jumped into the Jaguar. With Frank at the wheel they sped back down the road in search of Khoo and his daughter.

When they reached the main road they could see taillights vanishing rapidly to the south. Frank floored the accelerator to follow the speeding car but was unable to close the gap between them. Finally they lost sight of Khoo's car.

"Where now?" Frank asked. "Do you think they went to the Phoenix warehouse?"

"Too obvious," Joe said. "That place will be crawling with cops."

"Where else could they have gone?" Frank asked. "Home? No, they wouldn't risk that."

"I don't know," Joe said. "What about that antiques shop? The one that showed up in the photos we saw at the animal protection place?"

"Karl Bremer's place," Frank said. "You think they might have gone there?"

"You got a better idea?" Joe asked.

"Nope," Frank said. "Let's head for Bremer's."

They pulled up outside the antiques shop a few minutes later. The shop was located in a four-story building. The upper floors appeared to be a private residence. An alley ran next to the building. Although the antiques shop itself was closed, light shone through a window on the side of the building facing the alley, and dark figures could be seen moving around inside. Joe crept closer and recognized Jumsai Khoo and Ilsa.

He signaled Frank to peek through the window. Standing on a wooden box that was shoved against the side of the building, Joe peered into what appeared to be a large office. Sitting behind a massive antique desk was a man Joe assumed was Karl Bremer. He was seated directly across from the window, so Joe could see his face. He was about forty years old, with close-cropped blond hair and a heavily muscled body. His jaw was strong, and arrogance radiated from him.

Joe strained to listen to the conversation, but it was all in Swedish, so he couldn't tell what was being said. Standing across the desk from Bremer was Jumsai Khoo, who seemed to be arguing with Bremer. He kept pointing to his daughter, who sat quietly in a corner of the room, her forehead furrowed. She was obviously worried.

Why wasn't she speaking? wondered Joe. Was she involved in her father's schemes?

Bremer pressed a button, and a panel opened in the wall behind his desk. He extracted some papers that looked like a computer printout and briefly reviewed them. Then he picked up a telephone and made a call. Joe understood only two words: *Jumsai Khoo*.

Joe leaned forward to try to see more clearly. Suddenly there was a sound behind him, and he felt cold metal press against his neck.

It was the barrel of a gun. Inches away from his ear he heard a clicking sound. He knew that the next sound he heard might be his last!

Chapter

16

JOE AND FRANK whirled around to face the two men who had confronted them earlier in the basement of the Borsen Building. Both men were battered and bruised—not to mention quite angry at having had a pile of boxes dropped on top of them.

"Isn't this a coincidence?" said the blond. "I thought you were just two innocent kids who happened to stumble into our secret room."

"Hi, guys," Joe said with a weak smile. "I hope you don't have any hard feelings about that little incident."

"Hard feelings?" asked the other man. "No, we have no hard feelings. Which is why we're going to take you inside and introduce you to

Mr. Bremer. Of course, Mr. Bremer may be less than enthusiastic when he learns that you've been peeping through his windows. Nobody likes a Peeping Tom.''

"Hey, you must have us confused with somebody else," Frank said. "Neither of us is named Tom!"

"Very funny," said the man with the mustache. "Mr. Bremer will no doubt be highly amused by the two of you. Now get moving!"

"That's exactly what we plan to do," Joe said. "Get—*moving!*"

With a shout Joe dived off the box on which he was standing and grabbed the blond man by the throat. Startled by Joe's sudden movement, he fell backward, but as he fell he pulled the trigger of his gun. The bullet discharged into the air, whistling past Joe's ear. Joe slugged the blond man in the jaw, and he slumped to the ground.

Frank took advantage of the confusion and punched the other man in the stomach. The man staggered backward, and Frank punched him again, this time in the jaw. He collapsed across the inert body of his companion.

Joe stared down at the two unconscious men. "I hope this time they decide to take up another line of work. I'm getting sick of seeing these guys."

"Come on," Frank said. "Let's duck inside the antiques shop before that gunshot warns Khoo and Bremer away!"

The front door of the antiques shop was locked, but Frank forced it open with a strong kick. Inside they heard a babble of voices and the echoing of footsteps as Khoo, Ilsa, and Bremer raced toward the opposite end of the building. Frank and Joe ran through the antiques shop and opened a door in the rear just in time to see Bremer and his companions running down the alleyway in back. Khoo was headed in one direction, while Bremer and Ilsa were headed in another.

Joe followed Bremer and Ilsa. But before he could catch up with them Bremer raced onto a small dock and jumped into a speedboat. Ilsa jumped in after him, and the boat sped off. Joe looked around desperately for a boat that he could use to pursue them, but he could find none.

Frank, meanwhile, ran after Khoo. For a moment the older man ran as quickly as Frank, but then he turned down a blind alley. Blocked by a wall of trash cans and boxes, he had to face his pursuer.

"So," Khoo said, dropping into a karate pose, "you think you are good enough to do battle with me?"

Frank hesitated. Just then he remembered the gun that he had strapped to his ankle. He reached down and unstrapped it, the gun feeling odd in his hand. He had used guns rarely, but his father's death had changed the rules a bit.

Khoo was one of the people responsible for his father's death, and Frank felt no sympathy for him, no desire to offer him mercy. Frank started to point the gun at Khoo.

"I am disappointed in you, Frank," Khoo said. "That is not the way that honorable men do battle."

"Really?" Frank said. "Joe tells me that you pulled a gun on him back in the bell tower."

A shadow passed over Khoo's face. "That is true. Perhaps I am not always honorable myself, but I thought that you were."

Frank looked down at the gun. After a moment of deep thought he dropped it on the ground halfway between himself and Khoo.

"You're right," he said. "Guns aren't my style. Since they seem to be yours, I'll give you the chance to use this one. But you'll have to fight me for it."

Khoo bowed formally toward Frank. "I see that you are indeed an honorable man. I hope that you also prove to be a worthy opponent."

He stood perfectly still for a moment, as though gathering his inner resources. Then he dived forward with the litheness of a much younger man. Just before his hands closed on the gun Frank's foot lashed out and caught him on the shoulder. Khoo stumbled backward but did not lose his balance.

"Ah, you are fast!" he said. "That is good! Perhaps you are a worthy opponent. I wish that you had been able to accept my invitation to visit my dojo.''

Khoo smiled at Frank and became perfectly still again. This time Frank made the first move, lunging at Khoo and bringing his knees toward Khoo's stomach. But Khoo was ready for him. He grabbed Frank by the knee and flipped him over backward. Frank came down hard on his back, expelling his breath in a sharp gasp.

Khoo dived for the gun again, but Frank rolled into his path. Khoo stumbled over Frank but quickly regained his balance. But by this time Frank was back on his feet again.

The gun still lay between them.

"Very good!" said Khoo. "Very, very good! I would have defeated a lesser opponent by now. But you still cannot win. I will get the gun. You know that I will."

"I don't know any such thing," Frank said, fighting to catch his breath. "If you were that good, Khoo, you wouldn't need guns in the first place. You'd have kicked that gun away by now and demolished me with your bare hands. But you can't do it, and you know you can't do it."

Khoo's face fell. Frank knew that he had struck Khoo in the place where it hurt most, his pride. Khoo was proud of his prowess in the martial arts, but now he displayed a flash of anger at Frank.

Khoo dived for the gun one more time, but his anger affected his timing. Frank caught him on the jaw with his foot. Khoo staggered backward, then fell to the cobblestoned pavement.

He gazed up at Frank and gasped, "It is good—to fight with a worthy opponent."

Then he lapsed into unconsciousness.

"I called the police," Joe said when Frank found him in Karl Bremer's office. Frank had tied Khoo up and left him in the back of the antiques shop before going in search of his brother. "I hate to tell you this, but Ilsa and Bremer got away. I take it you took care of Ilsa's father?"

"Yeah," Frank told him. "He'll keep until the police get here. Meanwhile, let's take a look around this office, starting with that secret panel behind Bremer's desk."

Joe pushed the button that he had seen Bremer push earlier. The panel popped open, revealing stacks of computer paper inside.

Joe grabbed one of them and began reading. It appeared to be a list of antiques shops and clients who bought their products. Exactly the kind of thing that one would expect to find in the office of a high-powered antiques dealer.

Except—

The names on the list seemed to come from all over the globe, including Africa. Joe's eye automatically stopped at the listing of a client from Kenya who was supposedly visiting Stockholm and interested in antiques.

The client's name was Ezra Collig.

"Ezra Collig?" cried Frank. "That's Police Chief Collig's name, from back in Bayport. What would he be doing buying antiques in Stockholm?"

"Not a thing," Joe said. "I'm sure that Chief Collig is back in Bayport. Our police chief may be a lot of things, but a world traveler he isn't. And I've never heard him express the slightest interest in antiques."

"It's such an unusual name, though," Frank said. "Who else would use the name Ezra Collig?"

Joe's jaw dropped open, and he allowed the computer printout to fall back to the table. For a moment the whole room seemed to swim in front of his eyes, then he spoke the single word that had sprung into his head in answer to Frank's question:

"Dad!" he said.

"That's right!" Frank said. "Which would mean—"

"That Dad's still alive!" Joe exclaimed.

"Wait a minute," Frank said. "What's the date of the transaction listed on that printout?"

Joe scanned the list again and found the name Ezra Collig. The transaction had taken place one day after the explosion that had supposedly taken their father's life.

"I don't believe this," Joe said. "I don't know how Dad could have survived that warehouse fire, but I can't come up with any other way that the name Ezra Collig could have found its way onto this list.''

"Which means—" Frank started to say.

There was a pounding on the front door of the antiques shop. Frank left the office and opened the door. The police, Agent Fairchild, and a group of what appeared to be U.S. Intelligence officers walked into the store.

Frank led them to the room where he had left Jumsai Khoo. The man was beginning to stir, but when the intelligence agents began to question him, he refused to give them any information. Finally Fairchild motioned Frank and Joe back into Bremer's office.

"I don't know whether to lock you kids up or give you a medal," he said, scowling at the Hardys. "You did a good job catching Jumsai Khoo. That's definitely ten points for your team. But you chased away Karl Bremer—and who knows where he'll turn up again?"

"What's Bremer's involvement in all this anyway?" Frank asked.

"U.S. Intelligence has suspected for a long time that Bremer is involved with trafficking illegal aliens into the United States," Fairchild said. "But they haven't been able to pin anything on him. And of course, the fact that he's one of Phoenix's clients has always been more than a little suspicious, but we didn't know if he was involved with their smuggling operations. Until now."

One of the intelligence agents appeared at the

office door. "We're taking Khoo in for further questioning," he told Fairchild. "Want to come along?"

"You bet," Fairchild said. "Come on, boys. I'll give you a ride back to your hotel."

"We've got a car outside," Joe said.

"Which we have to return to Eleonora Grunewald," Frank added.

"I hope you've still got that police van you, ah, borrowed," Fairchild said. "The Stockholm cops are a little ticked off about the way you ran off with their equipment. And by the way, your friend Mike Ryan is going to be okay. The doctors tell me that he's really on the road to recovery."

"That's about the best news we've had all day," Joe said.

Fairchild and the Hardys exited through the front door of the antiques shop. Outside two of the intelligence agents were leading Jumsai Khoo toward a long black car.

Suddenly there was the sound of a gunshot in the air. Frank checked for the source, then saw Khoo clutch his chest and crumple to the street.

"Khoo's been shot," Fairchild said, looking around at the agents. "Where did that come from?"

Two of the agents raced down the street after a fleeing silhouette. They returned a few minutes later, dragging a familiar-looking swarthy figure between them.

Frank instantly recognized the man as Abdul Deharr, the same man who had been trying repeatedly to kill them over the last few days.

Fairchild was crouching over the still form of Jumsai Khoo. He felt the man's pulse for a moment, then let his hand drop back to the street.

"He's dead," Fairchild said. He turned to Deharr. "Who sent you to kill Khoo? I thought you worked for Khoo!"

Deharr was silent. Fairchild looked at him in disgust, asking him more pointed questions, but it quickly became clear that the terrorist had no intention of answering. Finally two of the intelligence agents led him into the dark vehicle that had been Jumsai Khoo's destination.

Joe stared down at Khoo's body. Frank put a hand on his brother's shoulder and realized that his hand was trembling.

Joe turned to his brother. "I don't believe this," he said. "Khoo is dead, Ilsa's missing, and Dad's out there somewhere in the middle of all of this."

"I wonder if even *Dad* hasn't bit off more than he can chew this time," Frank said. "Our father has never met a case he couldn't solve, but this may be the first time he's found himself in a maze of assassins as thick as this one."

"There's only one thing we can do," Joe said in a harsh voice. "We have to find Dad—before it's too late!"

Concluding Operation Phoenix:

The Hardys have come thousands of miles in search of their father's killers and will go to the ends of the earth to complete the job. From Stockholm to Copenhagen to Berlin, the trail is getting hotter by the minute—and their mission ever more critical. They've uncovered a shocking new piece of evidence: Fenton Hardy may be alive after all!

But the boys are working without a net, with no one to trust: not the beautiful Ilsa Khoo, not Interpol, not even the U.S. government. Someone inside the operation has betrayed the investigation, leaving Frank and Joe out in the cold. They'll have to go it alone and infiltrate Phoenix Enterprises no matter what the risks are. The time has come to face the truth and face the enemy . . . in *The Phoenix Equation,* Case #66 in The Hardy Boys Casefiles™.

Together for the first time!

The Hardys' sleuthing skills join with Tom Swift's inventive genius in a pulse-pounding new breed of adventure.

A
HARDY BOYS
AND
TOM SWIFT
ULTRA THRILLER™

TIME BOMB

A twist in time . . . A twisted mind . . .
A terrifying twist of fate for Frank
and Joe and Tom!

A dream that has long fired the human imagination has become a reality: time travel. But as Tom Swift and the Hardy boys are about to discover, the dream can become a nightmare in the blink of an eye. An attack force of techno-thugs, under the command of the evil genius, the Black Dragon, has seized control of a top-secret time-warp trigger!

Frank, Joe, and Tom leap into battle. But whether chasing asteroids or dodging dinosaurs, they know they haven't a moment to lose. They must stop the Dragon before he carries out his final threat: turning the time machine into the ultimate doomsday device!

Turn the page for your very special preview of . . .

TIME BOMB

"Detectors ready, Rob?" Tom Swift asked his robot assistant. "We have cosmic rays incoming in less than fifteen seconds."

The young, blond inventor gestured at the array of particle detectors that spread along the ridge they stood on.

Rob's glowing eyes gazed into the California desert sky. "Why did we power all this up so far in advance of the particle stream?"

"I want to catch some particles coming *ahead* of the rush," Tom explained.

"But cosmic rays move at the speed of light."

"Tachyons move faster," Tom said. "They'll show up twenty milliseconds before anything else."

"If they exist," Rob pointed out.

"In theory they do," Tom said. "Now we'll see if the universe is a democracy or a dictatorship."

"You've lost me, Tom," Rob said.

Tom's lean face lit up with a grin, and his deep-set blue eyes twinkled. "Either everything that's possible is allowed to happen—or everything possible *must* happen."

Rob read the data flying along the computer linkup. "I've picked up several particle anomalies in advance of the air shower created by the cosmic ray collisions."

The robot was silent for a moment. "It's as if the tachyons arrived *before* those collisions. Does that mean they traveled through time?"

Tom shrugged. "We all travel through time, Rob. What makes tachyons interesting is that they move in the opposite direction from us—"

The gleaming robot suddenly interrupted. "You've got a phone call."

Tom stared. "What?"

"It's a new improvement I was trying out, building your portable phone into my circuits. Just talk. My sensors will pick up."

A second later, Tom Swift, Sr.'s voice came through Rob's speakers. "Tom, are you there? I'd like you to come to my office. A rather interesting package has arrived."

"We're on our way." Tom and Rob started down the side of the ridge, to the van parked on the road below. They drove through the hills until they arrived at Swift Enterprises and made their way to Tom Swift, Sr.'s top-floor office.

Tom found his father at his desk. Mr. Swift took the wrapping from a flat box and handed it over. "What do you make of this?"

"It was sent by an S. Reisenbach." Tom frowned. "That's the name of the teacher you mentioned last night on that TV interview."

Tom's father nodded. "Ernst Reisenbach was one

of the most brilliant scientists of this century and one of the fathers of nuclear physics. During World War Two, he helped build the first atom bomb. Then Reisenbach was at Princeton for the next twenty years, teaching the next generation of scientists—including me."

He removed a letter from on top of the faded, dusty box in front of him.

" 'Dear Mr. Swift,' " he read aloud. " 'I listened with pride when you mentioned my great-uncle on "Up Front and in Person." We found this box, marked E. Reisenbach, while cleaning out the attic. When my husband and I saw you on TV, we decided that Uncle Ernst would have liked you to have his work.' "

Mr. Swift opened the box, to reveal a pile of yellowed papers covered with intricate math. As Tom's father followed the equations, his eyes grew large. "Reisenbach was years ahead when it came to theoretical physics. Here he postulates that besides the four dimensions we know—length, width, depth, and duration—there are seven other dimensions. These equations are for sending an object back along the space-time axis."

"That's ridiculous," Tom scoffed. "Unless he had a working time machine." He stared for a second, then dashed around his father's desk. "If Professor Reisenbach pulled *that* off, we ought to duplicate his experiments."

Three-thousand miles away in the east coast city of Bayport, Frank and Joe Hardy watched their father shake hands with a wiry man in a drab suit.

"This will be a different sort of case for me, Professor Drake," Fenton Hardy said, smiling. "Usually I trace criminals, not famous physicists."

"And usually I do not require the services of, ahem, private investigators to assist my research." Professor Drake peered over his half-glasses. "Dr. Reisenbach became a bit of a hermit after he left Princeton. His later years are shrouded in, well, mystery."

"How mysterious could a sixty-year-old professor get?" Joe Hardy's blue eyes gleamed impishly as he whispered to his older brother.

Frank Hardy ignored Joe's joking, a serious look on his lean features. "You think there's something mysterious in Dr. Reisenbach's papers?"

The professor shook his bald head. "The mystery is where those papers are." He handed a card to Fenton Hardy. "Here is my phone number. Good luck, and good hunting!" Drake shook hands with the boys and left.

For three days the Hardys banged their heads against a seemingly solid stone wall. "The guy is all over the public record till 1964," Frank complained. "Then he retires from the university, sells his house, cashes in all his investments, and *poof!* he's gone."

"Guys don't go *poof!* from May of one year to November of the next," Joe said.

"I think I can help with that," Fenton Hardy told them. "Dr. Reisenbach had a house in Canada. Technically, he still owns it. How would you like to check it out?"

"We've come pretty far in only two weeks." Tom looked at the mass of equipment that had taken over half of the Swift physics lab. Copies of Reisenbach's original designs were tacked on the walls, sometimes altered or completely revamped.

"It's amazing what he did with sixties technology," Mr. Swift said. "A working model of this thing would have taken up most of a house!"

"By substituting microchips for transistors, we've shrunk it down to manageable size," Tom admitted. "But it seems like a lot of work for a time machine that leaves you stranded in the past."

"We have only hints of that in Reisenbach's notes. Only testing will tell." Mr. Swift powered up the equipment. "Is the test material in place?"

Tom used a pair of tongs to set down a heavy lead bar. "All set, Dad. Is Harlan ready on the other end?"

"He's personally standing guard over his office safe," Mr. Swift said, grinning. "And he's wondering why I'm making him do that, since he knows the safe is empty." The smile faded. "Let's see if we can change that."

Tom joined his father behind a blast shield on the far side of the room. "All circuits are working," Mr. Swift reported, checking a set of gauges. "Energizing."

The hairs at the back of Tom's neck prickled as if an electrical charge had filled the air. He stared as a purplish glow suddenly surrounded the lead bar. "The field is forming," he said.

An indescribable sensation seized Tom, as if his body—or was it the world around him?—were being twisted. Everything went blurry.

Then the bar was gone.

Mr. Swift cut the power, his eyes glowing with excitement. "Let's get over to security," he said.

They reached Harlan's office to find him standing in front of his safe. "Let's see the inside," Mr. Swift said.

"I know what we'll see." The head of Swift Enterprises' security was a bit annoyed as he worked the dial. "Nothing. You made me remove— What the—?"

Harlan Ames whirled to stare at the Swifts. "What's that lead brick doing in there? I've been standing here since I emptied the stupid safe."

The Swifts grinned in triumph. They had sent the ingot back one minute into the past, aiming for the safe's coordinates.

"Don't tell me," Harlan said. "You invented some kind of cockamamie matter transmitter."

Laughing, Tom shook his head. "Even better, Harlan—a time machine."

Two days later, Harlan Ames still looked unhappy as he stared out the windshield of a Swift Enterprises' hovercraft. The all-terrain vehicle had whisked out onto the waters of the Pacific Ocean.

"Today we'll test the time trigger's capability for long-range travel," Mr. Swift told him. "Anchorage Rock is perfect for that purpose. No one has ever lived there, and according to our geological data, it was once considerably more low-lying than it is today."

"Is that why you had the team out there, digging a hole in the ground?" Harlan asked.

"We wanted to bring the time trigger as close as possible to the old level," Tom admitted. "The further back we send the test module, the less accurately we can place it spatially."

He vividly remembered what happened when they sent back a metal slug about the size of a nickel to appear in the center of a solid boulder. The result had been a huge blast—and a big hole in the ground where the boulder once stood.

"I was afraid that would happen," Mr. Swift had said. "It's the old problem of two objects trying to occupy the same space at the same time. If we're not careful in placing our time-traveling objects, they'll blow up, with one hundred percent energy efficiency."

Workers waved hello from the little U-shaped island as the hovercraft swung into a cove. Tom noticed that Harlan also had lots of security people in place.

With the help of the workers and some security people, they unloaded the prototype time machine.

"Set the test module," Mr. Swift said.

Tom swung down into the excavation, carrying a container about a foot long and four inches wide. Tom placed the module in the center of the time trigger, then climbed out of the way. If everything went right, the module would be flung back into the past.

A worried voice cut off their preparations. "Sir! Our sensors—they've gone dead!"

Harlan Ames leapt to the portable radio he'd taken from the hovercraft. "Perimeter guards!" he yelled. "Heads up!"

Even as Ames spoke, Tom heard the *thwip-thwip-thwip* of rotor blades as he ran for cover.

A moment later the helicopter came into view. It looked almost like a scale model, its body barely six feet long. It had to be under remote control. Either that, or the aircraft was a flying robot.

"Oh, no," Tom breathed. *"No!"* Only one man on Earth built robots like that. The Black Dragon!

The minichopper swooped into a curve, and a lance of fire darted from under its stabilizing wings. An attack rocket!

Tom whirled to see a figure rising from the water. He flung himself to take down his father and Harlan as the stutter of automatic gunfire filled the air. "Frogmen!" he yelled.

The Swift workers and security guards dropped to the sands. Many of them, though, didn't move.

"We're being massacred," Harlan said tightly. "Run for the hovercraft!"

Tom ran across the sands, his father right beside him. Two guards joined them, firing as they ran. Only one made it to the hovercraft.

Mr. Swift dove into the vehicle and started the engines. The hovercraft lifted off the ground on roaring fans. Harlan jumped aboard, and Mr. Swift piloted them away from the island.

Harlan stared back at the beach and the still figures there. "What about the ones who didn't make it?" he asked.

Either they're dead, or they've fallen into the hands of the Black Dragon." Mr. Swift's voice was bleak. "And so has the prototype time trigger."

Frank and Joe Hardy drove a rental car out of the Niagara Falls airport, heading for the Canadian side of the border.

They turned onto a small dirt path that wound under a canopy of dripping pine trees. The trees opened out into a small clearing, where a comfortably old-fashioned log cabin stood. It looked forlorn in the rain and was obviously not lived in.

Frank opened the car door. "There doesn't seem to be anybody around." He stepped over to the front window and peered in.

"But someone has been here," Joe said in a puzzled voice. He pointed at the damp ground in front of the cabin door. Frank saw footprints, tracks of a pair of stout boots heading away from the house.

"Well, he's gone now." Frank stood in the drizzling rain, an uneasy feeling in the pit of his stomach. "I think we should try to find the person who made those footprints. I'll get the car," he said.

They stopped at a gas station for a fill-up and some information. "Has anybody come through here lately?" Frank asked.

The young gas jockey thought for a second. "A guy in a blue pickup. Had this geezer riding along. He paid." The gas jockey laughed. "You should have seen his face when he saw what it cost."

"Can you give us a description?" Frank asked.

The gas jockey shrugged. "Old. Bald. White hair. Skin and bones."

"Did you notice which way the truck went?" Joe asked.

The gas jockey pointed toward town. "I heard the geezer say something about going to the library."

Frank looked at Joe. "What do you say we catch up on our reading?"

When they arrived at the library, they found a thin crowd, mainly older people stopping by for a look at the newspaper. One member of the sparse crowd, however, had no interest in current affairs. He sat in a corner, surrounded by encyclopedias, yearbooks, almanacs, and coffee-table books on the sixties, seventies, eighties, and nineties.

The man put a book down, and Frank stepped back, staggering. That weird feeling was back in the pit of his stomach, backed up with a chill down his spine.

He'd seen that face before, in books on the history of science.

The man was Ernst Reisenbach.

For days the Hardys and Dr. Reisenbach zigzagged across the country, surviving two encounters with the Black Dragon's robot attack force. Now, on a ridge overlooking Swift Enterprises, they had caught up with Tom Swift.

Tom stared at the older man, then declared to the Hardys, "That guy has to be a phony. The real Reisenbach disappeared thirty years ago. He'd be over ninety today."

"There are ways to hop over thirty years," Reisenbach said. He calmly ran a hand over the components of the time machine Tom had set up. "I am amazed at how *compact* you have made my apparatus. Miniaturization technology has certainly progressed since 1965."

Tom's mouth hung open for a second. Then he managed to say, "You—you mean to say you've created a machine that goes *forward* in time? All we've been able to construct is a machine that goes into the past."

"Ah," Reisenbach said. "I believe I know which papers fell into your hands, then. They only represented earlier stages of my work."

"Listen, we need to track down a time trigger,"

Tom said. "One was stolen by the Black Dragon—Xavier Mace. I've seen Mace pervert scientific discoveries into weapons of terror. Who knows what he'll do with a time machine?"

Harlan Ames was at the front gate when Tom and the others arrived at the Swift Enterprises complex.

"What was the big idea of going out alone?" Ames demanded, his face going red under his leathery tan. "We're supposed to be under full security, and you pull a fool stunt like that. Something's happened, and your father has been searching all over for you."

He glanced at the rental car. "And who are those people?"

"They're here to help," Tom said. "I'd better take them straight to Dad."

He whisked them straight to the administration building, and up the elevator to the top-floor office of Tom Swift, Sr. His father sat frowning behind his desk. "I hope you have—"

His voice ran out as he stared at Professor Reisenbach, standing behind Tom with the Hardys.

"Professor! Sir!" Tom senior was out from behind his desk, hurrying over to shake hands with Reisenbach. "How could you— Oh. You figured out how to come forward, too."

Reisenbach nodded, looking out the window and around the grounds of the Swift complex. "I congratulate you on how far you've come since your student days." Then a cloud passed over his features. "Now tell me about Xavier Mace."

Tom senior's face went grim. "I expect my son has told you that Mace succeeded in stealing our copy of your time machine." Reisenbach nodded, and Tom's father breathed a long sigh. "Now he's decided to use it, and the government has turned to me for help. Earlier this afternoon a metal box suddenly appeared from nowhere on the president's desk in the Oval Office. It simply materialized in a glow of purple light."

"The guy knows how to make an impression," Joe Hardy whispered to his brother.

"Inside the box was a videotape. Watch." Mr. Swift tapped a button. Immediately the wall opposite the desk began to glow as a floor-to-ceiling image appeared.

It was a man's face, with well-cut dark hair going gray, steady gray eyes, and slightly chubby cheeks that seemed chubbier as the man smiled.

Tom Swift recognized the face immediately as one of the many masks of the Black Dragon.

The image on the wall continued to smile. "Mr. President," Mace said in a pleasant voice. "As I'm sure you'll agree by the way this tape has appeared on your desk, I have developed an entirely new delivery system, for messages—"

Mace's smile disappeared. "Or weapons. I assure you, sir, that no amount of missile research or Star Wars technology can protect against it. My delivery system is a time machine."

For a second, a sneer passed over Mace's face, then he went on. "My proposal is simple. You are now the leader of the only superpower on Earth. Henceforth, you will confer with me on all policy matters, and I will have the final say. The world need never know." Mace's eyes went flat and ugly for a moment.

"You have one week to consider my proposal. If

you accept, merely arrange a press conference and use the words, 'A wise leader takes advisement from all quarters.' '' Xavier Mace smiled. "I will then arrange for regular communication."

Then the smile faded, and the face looking out from the wall was hard and unyielding. "If after a week you have not agreed, I shall have to give a more potent demonstration of my abilities. A more public demonstration, too."

Mace leaned forward, his eyes icy cold. "Somewhere in America a city will be destroyed—completely and utterly."

Want more?
Read the complete exciting story in

TIME BOMB

A Hardy Boys and Tom Swift Ultra Thriller™
Available July 15, 1992
Wherever Paperbacks Are Sold